What Should Have Been

By

Aurelia Yates

TABLE OF CONTENTS

ISBN-979-8-9910612-2-3

This book is dedicated to my late husband, Brent. I'll love you till my last breath.

Prologue

Paige

The ring of the doorbell alerts me that another guest has arrived. I'm a little jumpy, my nerves stretched tight, as people pour in for my eighteenth-birthday party. I place my hands on my stomach, which feels as though a train is speeding through it, ripping it apart.

When Mom dropped the bomb on me about the gathering she had arranged, I asked who she'd invited. She named friends, family, and people I'm not even sure I know.

The dress I bought yesterday to wear tonight is not a style I'd usually wear, but I really want to make an impression on a certain person. I'm optimistic this dress will get the reaction I'm wanting. If it doesn't, then I'm going to start thinking I'm the problem.

I step into the royal blue satin dress and shimmy it up and over my flared hips, before pulling the thin straps up to lay smoothly on top of my sun kissed shoulders. The short dress has a hugging bodice that exposes the top of my chest. I just hope I'm not revealing too much. Being a conservative girl, I wouldn't normally wear anything that would show a hint of cleavage but tonight is a special occasion. When I reach behind, I tug lightly at the zipper and close it with ease, molding the fabric to my figure.

Grabbing the shoe box from my bed, I open it. The nude heels that are tucked neatly inside are individually wrapped in a protective plastic keeping them safe from getting scuffed up. Lucky for me, I have kept these looking like new and didn't have to purchase new shoes to go with my dress. I slip them on and look at myself in the mirror — they complement the dress perfectly!

The person staring back at me in the full length mirror isn't the same girl I've been looking at every day for the past eighteen years. Nope. She's not a girl anymore. She's a woman. I almost don't recognize myself. I smile at my reflection and take a moment to admire my perfectly straight teeth. I send a silent thank you to the dental gods that my hideous metal braces were finally removed earlier this week.

I turn to my side, pushing out my chest. When my breasts decided to make an appearance this year, I cried tears of joy. I was flat chested for so long that I didn't think they would ever develop. Cute tops that had a low V-neck had been out for me. They just didn't seem to fit right on my small chest. My friend Kellie on the other hand… Well let's just say she could wear a garbage sack and there still wouldn't be enough coverage for her boobs.

Before heading down to the party, I twirl in front of the mirror one last time, admiring my outfit, hoping for the happy ever after ending that I've imagined for tonight.

When I leave my bedroom, I walk with ease. It's almost

painful to hold back my excitement and not sprint down the stairs to find Cain, but I maintain my composure.

Cain and I have been dating since last summer and then he went off to college over two hours away. We did the best we could to keep our relationship intact but since we were limited on the time we could spend together, things between us have become strained. I'm hoping that now that he's home for the summer and I'll be joining him at college in the fall, we'll be able to seal up those cracks and make a stronger foundation.

My steps halt on the last step of the staircase when I spot Cain across the living room. He's dressed in a pair of ripped jeans and an old eighties band t-shirt. His long-ish hair is tousled to perfection. It's the epitome of the bad-boy-with-good-boy-morals archetype that makes your mouth water.

His style now is different than it was before he went off to college. He used to dress in polo shirts and kept his hair shorter. I can tell there's been a change in him. His posture and the way he gestures are more confident. I guess going off, living with a houseful of frat boys, will do that to someone. His deep laugh brings me out of my foggy mind.

My friends are huddled around him, flirting. I can see the envy in their eyes knowing that he's mine. When Kellie says something, he throws his head back laughing, his eyes meet mine, and it feels like my whole world just stops. Everyone around us fades out of the picture. My eyes dip down to his moving lips. I can't hear him or read his lips. And then he's taking smooth, measured steps in my direction, making my heart flip a million summersaults. When he reaches me, he gives me his killer smile—the one that stretches across his full lips displaying his perfect white teeth.

God, he's so divine.

"Hey Paige," he says with a hint of seduction.

"Hey," I reply breathlessly.

It should be a crime for him to look as beautiful as he does. He's breathtaking in every way imaginable. His hair, his teeth, his long legs, and a smile that could woo anyone into giving him what he wants—the whole package is ungodly wicked.

We drift over to a dimly lit corner where we can be alone. I grab a piece of my dress's skirt in my hands. They're shaking as the words play over and over in my mind. I want tonight to be my first time, I just need to say it. He's been understanding of me waiting till I felt ready to give myself to him. I just need to get my courage up to say it.

Cain and I have known each other since I was fourteen. I shouldn't be this nervous. I've always been able to say, do, or tell him anything. So why can't I just come out and say it? Maybe, I'm not ready.

"You look nice." He compliments me as his eyes shine.

"Thank you."

I sink a little inside. *Nice.* What does that even mean? I look nice like best friend nice? I look nice as in I look like crap most of the time? I want to look more than nice to him. I want Cain to think I'm the sexiest woman he's ever seen.

Opening my mouth, I start to tell him that I want him, but before the words can form he holds up a finger and looks off toward the kitchen, stopping me from speaking.

"Wait here. I'll be right back." He walks off without letting me get a word out.

I watch his back as he disappears into the kitchen. After several minutes standing there, waiting on him to return, I decide I need to speak to my other guests.

There are bubbles of agitation in my stomach and I desperately wish I could pop them to make them go away. Surely, I can't expect Cain to stay by my side the entire time, so why am I feeling upset? I huff at my own thoughts as I try to reason with myself. Yes, I do want him to want to be at my side. I want him to wrap his arm around my waist and lead me through the room. I want him to show all my friends and family he wants a bond with me just as much as I want it with him.

Looking down at myself, I try to gauge what he saw. *Nice. You look nice, he said.* Something about that irritates me. *I look better than nice. I look sinful, ready to be devoured.*

A deep voice speaks in my ear, "Hey." My knees almost give out with the sound of it. "Paige," he gasps. "You look breathtakingly beautiful."

My mouth goes dry. Maybe he realized how he made me feel earlier. I try to hide my emotions, but my mother has always said my facial expressions give me away.

"Thank you," I say so low it's almost a whisper. "You changed your clothes."

"Hmm," he replies.

He reaches out and slides his hand into mine, gently stroking my knuckles with his thumb. His touch feels different but right, like how it should have felt all along. The sizzle from of our skin touching rushes through my veins, sending tingles down my spine. God, I wish we were the only two people in the room. I could get lost in this moment, in the way those beautiful gray eyes gaze down at me.

He's never held my hand for so long, touched me in such an adoring manner. My mind is blown from the simple touch.

It makes me want to close my eyes, willing his soft touch to trail over my skin. I need more of his tender strokes, I want more and I'm hoping he'll give me what I desire tonight.

Nervously, I pull him closer and whisper, "I want you tonight. I want you to be my first."

He's quiet, so quiet that I begin to doubt myself for saying anything at all. I can see emotions swirling in his eyes. I want to believe it's love and not lust that I see.

Pulling me into his body, he wraps his arms around me. He holds me tight, as he breathes me in.

"I'll sneak in tonight, leave your window unlocked for me," he says as he presses his lips against mine in a soft, tender kiss that makes my toes curl. "I love you, Paige. It'll only ever be you. You're the only one I'll ever love." His words fill my ears and steal the air from my lungs. It's one of those moments that will be forever stamped in my mind. It's the first time those words were ever spoken to me.

The rest of the night doesn't compare to that kiss. I give my aunt and uncle one last hug before they leave. It's almost midnight when we get done cleaning up.

"I can finish the dishes in the morning. Go on and head to bed sweetie." My mom says, exhaustion showing in her face. "Happy birthday, baby." She gives me a kiss on the cheek.

"Good night, Mom. Thank you for a wonderful party."

When I open my bedroom door, the room is dark with only a small bit of moonlight shining around the edge of the curtains. I decide to leave the lamp off and take a moment for my eyes to adjust to the darkness. When I close the door someone speaks.

"Hey."

Startled, I jump and bump my back up against the door.

"Oh my heavens you scared me."

He chuckles, sending me into a foggy state. That sound he makes, it's more of a feeling of walking on clouds. I want to lose myself and float on his laugh, his whispers, but most of all just him.

"I didn't mean to scare you." He rushes to me, taking me into his arms and holding me close—pressing my heart to his.

"It's fine. I was just so tired I didn't realize you might be in here already."

I can't see his eyes but I feel them on me.

"We can do this another time," he offers.

We could, but you only turn eighteen once, and I'll only lose my virginity once.

"No, I… just give me a few minutes to use the bathroom."

He places his finger under my chin, raising my face up. His soft full lips press against mine.

"I'll wait right here," He says after the tender kiss.

"Okay." I'm barely able to get the word out.

Making my way to the adjacent bathroom, I flip on the light. Turning back, I take in the boy sitting in the shadows on my bed. I'm about to give all of myself to him and my body is humming.

"Could you lock the door?" I point to the bedroom door. My room is at the very end of the hallway and it's above the kitchen. Since my sister Pace's room is above my parents' room, at the other end of the hallway, the chance of them hearing anything is slim. I just need to make sure Pace won't be able to come in if she hears us.

I close the bathroom door to undress and freshen up, but once I'm ready I decide to put my dress back on. Nerves are getting the best of me, though, because I can't decide if I need to leave the dress on or take it off. Then I say forget it. I'll leave it on.

One hand on the doorknob and the other on the light switch, they race to see which one can beat the other to do their job. My right hand wins by opening the door faster. My left one is about to turn off the light but it doesn't finish the race. Because there he is, his chest faintly illuminated by the dim light spilling from the bathroom, laying in my bed with the sheet barely covering what he's offering me tonight.

My eyes strain to see every muscle, every strand of blond hair scattered across his beautiful chest. Unable to help myself, my gaze stops on the tented sheet, worried by the size of the stake that's holding it up. It's larger than what I would have thought.

"Are you enjoying the view?" His amusement is obvious in the tone of his voice.

"Maybe. Or maybe I'm trying to decide if you are worth my troubles," I say, trying to give him shit.

He pulls the sheet back and I swear my eyes almost pop out of my head at the size of his cock. I've never seen one before, but still—I definitely never thought they could be so… large. There's a birthmark on his abs, just above his cock, in the shape of Texas. All it needs is a star and it would be the perfect emblem for the state.

He slides his legs off the bed, stands, and walks to me. I cannot take my eyes off his cock. I stand there with my chest rising with each breath and my hormones going wild. His manhood is too much and I'm wondering if I'll be able to take him.

He places his hand over my left one, which is still gripping the light switch, and together we turn off the light. "You may be less anxious if we do this with only the moonlight." His arms wrap around my waist. "Whatever you're thinking, don't overthink it." His lips start their soft attack on my neck. He rubs his nose along my neck and then back up behind my ear. I moan and his hands quickly move to cover my mouth.

"Shhh." He uncovers my mouth. "You have to be quiet. Your dad will kill me if he finds me in your room," he whispers.

"Oh sorry." I whisper back.

"Turn around."

I turn my back to him and he pulls all my hair together, and then lays it over my shoulder on one side. His fingers work their magic unzipping my dress and I lower my arms so it'll fall to the floor. A small growl of appreciation leaves his throat and I praise myself for buying the new set of underclothes I'm wearing. His fingers brush my exposed neck, before softly trailing down my spine to the top of my g-string. When his fingers dip into the elastic band he rips it off of me, making me gasp.

"Don't worry baby. I'm going to handle you with care," he breaths into my ear.

Soon after ripping my g-string off, he unfastens my bra and it follows my dress to the floor, laying next to it. His arms wrap around me, each of his hands grabbing a breast and squeezing. When he pulls me back into him, I feel his hard cock rubbing against the crack of my ass.

"Turn around, face me," he orders.

When I turn around I watch his head tip down to scan my body. I feel exposed, even my heart feels too exposed for him to view. I'm thankful, for a moment, that Cain turned off the light, but even so my insecurities about my body make me want to jump under the sheet.

I finally get the courage to speak. "Say something." His approval is the validation I need.

"You're perfect."

CHAPTER ONE

Paige

Six Years Later

Orange Beach in Alabama has been one of my favorite vacation spots for almost as long as I can remember. Growing up, I visited this same spot with my husband's sister, Callie. Callie's been my best friend since middle school.

I'm lying on my stomach on a beach towel, my feet extended past its edge so I can dig my toes into the tiny grains of soft, white sand. The large colorful umbrella provides me with enough shade to enjoy the suspense novel in my hand without having to squint my eyes. This is the relaxing atmosphere I look forward to every year.

The ocean breeze picks up, covering me with a blanket of warm air. Inhaling the salt air and staring out at the vast, never-ending body of water is something that I never get tired of. It provides a sense of peace to my soul.

Now that Cain and I have a family, we keep the tradition alive by coming to the beach each year. Our children love building sand castles, burying their daddy in the sand, and playing with him in the water.

I hear laughter coming from the direction of the crashing waves and look up from my book. That sound—my children's laughter mixed with their father's, never grows old.

Our children, Jameson who is one and Ivory who's three, adore their father. He's so eager to be a part of their lives, spoiling them with attention. Cain has always made our children a priority, putting their needs ahead of his.

Children have always tugged at Cain's heart strings. It's one of the reasons why he chose a career as a teacher and one of the many things we have in common—I chose the same career because of my love of children as well.

We're both teachers at the public school in our small community. I teach the primary grades while Cain teaches ninth grade history—but it's his coaching work that he enjoys the most. When the junior football head coach position was offered to him, he couldn't sit still for weeks because he was so excited. His time for us becomes thinner during the season but I know how much he loves his students. He gives them as much care as he gives his own family. No one could be a better role model than he is.

"Hey, babe," my husband calls as he splashes the kids, "come get in the water."

"In a minute," I yell back and return to my book, wanting to finish the chapter.

When I feel water dripping on my shoulder, I glance up at my husband's handsome face, smiling at me. His smile is contagious and spreads to my lips.

When I remember the children, I sit up in a rush. He was just with them in the water.

"Where are the children?"

He drops to his knees. "Relax," he coaxes. "They're right there." He points to the direction where the children are, just a few feet from us.

They're playing in the sand and the sun bounces off their sun protection tops. Being like any other mother, my heart swells, because they are my pride and joy.

I lay back down on my towel and Cain joins me, peppering wet kisses on my shoulder.

He whispers into my ear, "Come in the water to play with me."

I roll on my back, and he spreads his large palm on my stomach. After having children I'm still uncomfortable with him placing his hand there. I don't feel as secure with my body as I did before pregnancy. I gave up wearing certain articles of clothing that felt too tailored because of my own insecurities. It's amazing how much my body changed after I had our children but I would give up an hour-glass figure any day for my babies.

"You're so beautiful," he whispers.

"You're not going to give up until I get up, are you?" I purse my lips.

"Not at all." He gives me his breathtaking smile.

"Fine."

I jump up and take off running toward the water, hearing Cain laughing behind me. The sand kicks up on the back of my legs with each stride I take. Before I'm able to get to the ocean the sky grows black. A dark cloud has passed in front of the sun but instead of actually passing over us, it hovers... staying in place. What felt like a day of promise has become a day of dread.

With every step I take toward the water, it draws back, causing me to come to a complete halt and stand there, befuddled. The once clear blue ocean transforms into a sea of blood, staining the white grains of sand as it's sucked away, as if it's running from me. When I look back at Cain, he's nowhere in sight. Panic seeps into my bones, and I run frantically searching for him and the children. My head turns left and right trying to find them but they're no where.

The plastic toys lay in the sand where the children were playing just seconds ago. In slow motion, one by one people start disappearing in front of my eyes. Soon, there's no one on the beach except me. I'm left alone. All alone. I let out a pain-filled scream.

I bolt upright in bed, beads of sweat running down my forehead. My heart thrashes in my chest. As I glance around the barely lit room, I realize I'm in my bedroom.

Oh God, it was a dream.

I lie back down and close my eyes. My chest heaves with each breath. I do my best to calm myself, intentionally taking in slow breaths and exhaling. I need to relax. Cain doesn't need to feel my tension, he's had to deal with so much in the past year.

Last summer, on our annual beach trip, our lives were changed in the blink of an eye. One moment we were walking out of a restaurant, laughing and enjoying the evening, and then the next, Cain had collapsed with a seizure.

Callie and her husband had joined us for dinner that night and thank goodness she is a nurse because she knew exactly what to do. I've never been so grateful to have her by me as I was the moment his eyes started rolling and his body shaking. While she took over making sure he didn't swallow his tongue or bite it, I escorted the children away. I didn't want them to be frightened. He wouldn't have wanted them to see him like that.

When the ambulance rushed into the parking lot, I handed the children off to their Aunt Callie while I loaded up with Cain for the short ride to South Baldwin Regional Medical Center in Gulf Shores. As we sped through the night, I prayed for the strength for us to meet whatever this was head on. His fate, our fate, was waiting for us, like an unwanted surprise that couldn't be returned.

We waited what felt like days before we were given the results of the tests the hospital had run. I held on to hope that the seizure was caused from being dehydrated. Even when I tried to will the doctors to say what I wanted to hear, I knew in my heart it wasn't going to happen.

Those three words *stage four cancer* still echo in my ears like it was only minutes ago that I heard them for the first time. They were like a curse dooming us to a life I had no idea how to maneuver through.

Anxiety crashed into me, leaving me panting for air. I couldn't breathe. I couldn't think straight. All I could wonder was, *why?* Why did this happen to him? To us? To our young children that need their father for life's biggest challenges.

Sometimes I wonder what would have happened if we had stayed home instead of going on vacation. Would he have had a seizure? Would they have diagnosed him with the tumor on his brain? Would our future be sealed with this expiration date we're creeping toward?

When Cain was released from the hospital in Gulf Shores, we were referred to a team of specialists four hours away in Birmingham. They took up the task of giving us directions on the options available to us, but very little was said about hope for a miracle as they spoke. Cain had been diagnosed with glioblastoma. A brain cancer that is not curable. If there had been a window for treatment, we had missed it. The cancer had already spread down his spine to his lungs, kidneys, and liver.

I remember looking over to Cain, watching him as the doctor's voice made white noise in the background. All I could do was focus on his face and how it fell. He looked so helpless. I recall reaching out to hold his hand and bringing it up to my lips to kiss it, wishing I could bottle up his pain and bury it instead of him.

CHAPTER TWO

Paige

My breathing and heart rate somewhat back under control after the nightmare, I reach over to the other side of the bed and rub the empty pillow. Rolling to my side, I bury my face into it, inhaling a deep breath as I try my best not to breakdown.

The smell of Cain's cologne is embedded into the soft cotton pillowcase. Even after all the months he hasn't slept in our bed, I still can't bring myself to strip his pillowcase from the pillow and wash it.

Sadness pours into my pores when I think about happier times. How we felt so blessed. I'm nothing like the happy person I used to be. I'm only the outer shell of the person who pretends everything is going to be okay as I try to make it through each day, faking the smiles that I put on to hold myself together, to be good enough for our children.

Mourning the life we lost before Cain's illness, I close my eyes feeling so selfish for wanting it back. I should be grateful for each day we have left together. My eyes squeeze tighter, wringing a tear loose. It falls away—forgotten, just like my blessings.

Be more grateful, Paige!

When faint breathing reaches my ears, I open my eyes and look over at the hospital bed in our room. I focus on the seconds between each breath. Cain's breathing has changed yet again. Each day it grows more shallow, each breath shorter. I know his time here is rapidly coming to an end, and grief fills me to the core. I've loved this man since I was seventeen, built my world around him. How will I ever get past his death?

Unable to lie here any longer and indulge in my usual morning pity party, I throw the warm covers back, then slip my feet out of bed and into my slippers. I mentally prepare myself before I start my routine. Having a set schedule for every day is the only norm to my life right now. It makes me feel like I have some control in my day-to-day routine.

My day starts with ensuring Cain is comfortable and his bedding is dry. After checking, I kiss his clammy forehead.

"I love you," I whisper in his ear. Every morning and every night I express my love for him.

He doesn't open his eyes. When I join our hands together, he gives me a small squeeze. Holding his hand, I stroke his hair back with the other.

"You need a haircut. I need to see if Kellie will come and cut it for you."

When I talk to Cain, I do my best to include the topics we would normally have discussed—even though our everyday life is now so far from normal. Our normal disappeared last year. Treating him differently, though, would only leave him feeling defeated, like he is a burden to me. But taking care of him has never felt like a weight holding me down. He's in there, I can feel it. The small squeeze he gives me, tells me he hears me. I know he does.

When I witnessed Cain's seizure, I'd never been so scared

in my life. The shaking of his body, the foam coming from his mouth, and the voidness in his eyes, thank goodness we were with Callie and she knew exactly what needed to be done. His neurologist said that wasn't his first seizure because the high-density electroencephalogram he had confirmed that he'd had seizures before that day.

Cain had never spoken of having any previous attacks but the doctor had said it was very possible he'd had no idea they had occurred. The doctor said that a seizure does not always involve the patient swallowing or biting their tongue and there's a good chance Cain didn't add up the signs that could have led us to getting everything identified sooner. I beat myself up often, wondering how I could have missed the signs of there being a problem.

Cain's breathing stops, and the heart monitor's alarm starts making the "flat line" sound. The fear of losing him becomes more of a reality every second. I quickly grab the phone and dial 911. I give the dispatcher our address and the details she needs, and she dispatches an ambulance. The whole time we're waiting I give him CPR, hoping it's enough.

The ambulance arrives, the paramedics take over, and before I know it, they have a slow heartbeat. After they've rushed out the door to take him to the hospital, I change my clothes and hurry into the kids' rooms to get them up. I'm not concerned about changing them out of their pajamas— my only fear is not getting to Cain before he leaves us.

Not even thirty minutes later, we arrive at the hospital and wait in the emergency room. I patiently sit with the kids. My hands shake as I dial my sister's number. The phone starts to ring and I kiss the top of my son Jameson's head. At two, he's more of a mama's boy than he was last year. He's sitting on my lap while Ivory, his big sister, lies across several seats, her head pressed against my leg.

"Paige, is everything okay?" Pace's voice is shaky.

Pace knows that Cain's time is quickly coming to an end, and worry consumes her almost as much as it does me. I can hear in her voice that she's worried that I'm calling to report the news of his death.

"Pace, I'm back at the emergency room. I need you to come and get the kids for me."

"What happened?" Concern laces her tone.

"Nothing. Just a little scare," I say. I don't want to worry my family or Cain's and I don't want my children to hear me talk about their father dying.

"Yeah, I'm on my way." I hear her rustling in the background, and I know she must still have been in bed. Pace is five years younger than me and even though she is still at the party stage, I can depend on her to watch the kids.

She calls me when she arrives outside the hospital. I walk the kids out to load them up in her small two-door car. I take in the small backseat and worry that if she has a wreck the kids would be crushed to death.

"Why don't you take mine? It'll save me from taking out the kids' seats," I suggest, hoping she'll agree.

"Sure."

She pulls her car over to park beside mine and I remember to be grateful the parking lot is mostly empty at this early hour. I hurry to buckle the kids up. Kissing their sweet faces, I tell them how much Daddy and I love them.

I watch Pace drive off and then, as I look at the sliding doors I'll have to walk through to get back in, dread washes over me. Now, I have to go inside and face what is happening with Cain. On my way to his room, nausea hits me. I run into the nearest restroom and huddle over the toilet. Everything in my stomach is coming back up and out in a rush. When I'm done, I prop myself up against the wall, feeling like my life is being drained from me.

Giving myself a pep talk in the mirror, I say, "Come on, Paige, you can do this."

But I can't. I can't do this. Tears fill my eyes, and the feeling of being alone, without the man I was supposed to spend the rest of my life with, slams into my heart. I take in a deep breath and exhale.

I am strong, I am strong.

Repeating the words that have gotten me through this past year, I splash my face with water and head to Cain's cubicle in the emergency room.

When I arrive, I observe his pale color and how he looks like he's barely hanging on. They have him on a bi-pap machine. Wires and tubes are attached to him, and I wonder if all the wires and tubes are doing more harm than good. A knock on the wall startles me out of my thoughts. When I turn, I see Dr. Gordon's face peering around the curtain as he steps into the small room.

"Hey Paige," he greets me.

Dr. Gordon is Cain's oncologist and a close friend of ours. This past year, we've seen so many doctors, so it's nice to have a close friend who is personally invested in Cain's health.

"Gordon, how is he?" I ask.

"It doesn't look good. His oxygen levels are low. We have him on the bi-pap, but it's not bringing his levels up to where we would like them." He pauses and puts a hand on my shoulder. "If we put him on the ventilator it will do his breathing for him—but honestly, Paige, I'm not sure if that would be the best thing for *him.* You really need to prepare yourself and decide, are you trying to do the best for him or are you doing what you want by trying to keep him here. We've done everything that is available to us. All the treatments and surgeries that are appropriate have been performed. It's up to you if you want to keep trying but eventually you can't stop what is unavoidable."

My body goes numb, my mind goes blank, and darkness blocks my vision.

When I slowly blink my eyes open, there are four strangers looking down at me. I'm lying on the hard surface of the emergency room floor. Dr. Gordon and three nurses are standing over me. All my energy has left my body. I don't have the strength to answer the questions they are asking. There is chaos surrounding me but I'm not understanding anything at this moment. It's all beyond my comprehension.

Someone lifts me into a chair, hands me a bottle of water, and I take a sip, letting my gaze flow over to Cain. I need to make the call. The call I've been trying to fool myself into believing I wouldn't have to make.

Wait, I'll wait. I need to wait. They don't know. Doctors don't know everything.

CHAPTER THREE

Paige

Every word the doctor said had broken a little more of my heart. *You can't stop the unavoidable.* Thinking of the past, when we were our happiest, when Cain was healthy, makes me want to hold on with both hands. The decision to not put Cain on the ventilator tore my soul apart. Letting him go has been the toughest decision I've ever had to make. I know in my heart everything has been done to try and make him stronger. Trying to keep him with us is too selfish when I know how weak his body is.

We were moved into a comfort suite in the west wing. All the wires and tubes have been removed and Cain is laying in his hospital bed looking peaceful. I die a little bit more inside listening to him barely breathing. It's just a matter of hours, maybe minutes, before he'll be free from the cancer. The dreadful cancer that has consumed his body in the worst way.

It's too quiet with it just being me and Cain, so I open the door, hoping chatter from the nurse's station will bring life to the oppressive stillness filling the air. The silence has spun me deep into the reality that Cain is leaving me and loneliness has seeped into my bones.

My hand is unsteady as I fumble for my phone in my purse and then dial my sister's number.

"Paige," Pace whispers into my ear.

"Will you please bring the kids so they can say goodbye? And call Mom and Dad and let them know. I need to call Cain's family."

"We're on our way… Paige?" Her voice is soft when she speaks my name.

"Yes?"

"You're strong. You're going to get through this. Everyone is here for you. Whatever you or the kids need don't hesitate to ask. I love you sissy."

"I love you." My body trembles when I end the call.

Swiping away the tears that escape my eyes, I take a breath, steadying myself as I dial Cain's parents. My heart feels like it's about to beat out of my chest. No parent wants to hear the words I'm about to say.

When we were children, life didn't appear this difficult. I can't help but wonder what I did to deserve my husband getting sick and dying at such a young age. We're only in our twenties. This is when we should be raising our family and mapping out the future we're looking forward to, not making funeral plans.

Cain's mother picks up the phone, asking "Paige, is it Cain?" I can hear her sorrow and feel her pain through the phone.

I do my best not to break down and cause her more pain.

"Yes, we're in room W512. They took him off the breathing machine. You need to come now. I don't know how much longer he will last."

I try my best to be strong, although *strong* is the last thing I feel right now. I want to be a little girl again and let my parents wrap me up in their arms and kiss my boo-boos away. Sadly, I'm an adult in this nightmare and I have to be strong enough for my children.

"Will you call Callie for me?" I quietly plead.

I can't bear to tell my childhood friend that her brother is dying, especially since we just learned that she and her husband Jack are finally pregnant.

"I will, sweetie." She pauses. "You know you are family. You'll always be family."

My eyes pool with tears. "Thank you. I never thought differently."

We hang up with her words still ringing in my ears. *You'll always be family.*

It doesn't take long for Pace to show up with the children. As soon as they walk into the room, I feel the lingering gloomy cloud lift off me. They run to me, engulfing me in their light. Wrapping my arms around them, I want to shield them from this dreadful moment. I want to make sure their last moments with their dad are a wonderful memory, not one of sadness.

I look at my children, noting all of the features they received from their dad's side of the family. The golden skin, their gray eyes.

With my arms still wrapped around them, I ask, "Do you want to go give Daddy love?"

Jameson hesitates, shakes his head, and buries it into my neck. Ivory looks frightened, but slowly walks over to Cain, reaching for his hand. She puts her head on his shoulder, speaking so low I can't hear what she's saying.

I almost lose it. The sight of Ivory with her head resting on his shoulder makes my heart swell with pride. Then the thought that this will be the last time she rests her head on his shoulder—it kills me.

Feeling tears drip off my chin, I quickly swipe them away.

I turn Jameson's face to look at me. I want him to say goodbye to his dad. I'm afraid if he doesn't go over to give him a hug, he will want to later and won't have the chance.

"Jameson, go give Daddy a hug."

He shakes his head with force. Then plants his face back into my neck.

"Why do you not want to?" I ask softly.

He mumbles something into my neck and I'm not able to understand him. Gently tugging him by the shoulders, I pull him back to look at me.

"Tell me again. Why don't you want to?"

Little teardrops run down his face. "He's leaving us. Why doesn't he stay?"

I close my eyes and take a deep breath. How can you tell your almost three-year-old that it's not his father's choice? I do my best and explain that if Daddy had his way, he would stay, but sometimes things happen, and you must accept them.

After speaking to Jameson for fifteen minutes, he finally walks over to the bed. I lift him close to his father and he throws his short arms around Cain's neck, squeezing it.

"It's okay, Daddy. We'll see you soon," Jameson says loudly.

I sniff. Try my best not to lose it. My eyes move around the room and see all of our loved one's have arrived and gathered around. It sends my heart soaring.

Cain makes a noise and I quickly reach for the children, pulling them into my lap. I need them close to me. They're just as much my rock as I have to be their rock now.

The nurse walks over to check Cain's vital signs. I watch her as she listens for a heartbeat and takes his pulse. She looks up at me and shakes her head. He's passed on. I don't cry. I don't feel any emotion. Numbness runs throughout my body. I cling to my children; protecting them is my number one priority now.

My sister's hand lands on my shoulder and my mother's arms wrap around me from the back.

Mary, Cain's mother, walks over. "Go home, Paige, take the kids, and get some rest. We'll take care of everything from here."

I nod. The single tear that's been hanging on to my eyelash drops to my cheek.

"Thank you." I hold my hands away from my sides—Ivory slides her hand into my right one and Jameson takes my left hand. Together we walk over to Cain's bed and I bend to kiss Cain's cheek, whispering in his ear, "I'll always love you."

I'll always love you is what he said to me every night when he crawled into bed.

CHAPTER FOUR

Paige

It's four days later, and I'm sitting on the edge of the bed staring out the window. A bird flies straight at me, crashing into the window, and I don't even flinch. I'm too lost in my mind to even care about the poor creature that is probably laying on the grass, flapping his wings. I think about the bird and remember an old saying I used to hear. *A death will occur when a bird hits a window.* Ironically, it's already happened.

The bed dips beside me.

"The kids are dressed," Pace whispers. "It's going to be okay, Paige." Her hand rubs my upper back.

Why does everyone keep telling me that?

Everything is not going to be okay. They don't have to come back to this house. They don't have to look at each piece of furniture and every picture that hangs on the walls. The memories of trying to fit the oversize furniture into tight spaces because Cain forgot to measure the space beforehand.

Then there are the memories of the kids. Jameson having diarrhea and ruining the carpet and Ivory's dress. Then

Ivory's crying fit because she had poop on her. Cain's laughter at the chaos made the potentially traumatizing event lighter.

His patience, laughter, and smile brightened up every hectic moment.

My shoulders sink when I think about having to come back here without him. It's happened before, of course, when he spent nights in the hospital. But today it just feels… final—in some weird way, even more final than these last few days when he's been at the funeral home. My head bows so far down it almost touches my lap.

This can't be my life.

Pace wraps her arm around me and I uncurl enough to lean on her shoulder.

"Let's go grab the kids and head out. Mom and Dad are going to meet us there."

I nod and stand, then walk to the window to check on the bird. It struggles a bit but finally stands on his feet. I can only hope that it's a sign.

I turn, grab my purse, and walk toward my bedroom door with Pace behind me. The children come bouncing in before we make it out.

"Mommy, can we get ice cream?" Ivory asks enthusiastically.

She's too small to fully understand today. How it's not a day of celebrating by grabbing ice cream but a day to say goodbye to her daddy. I don't get upset. I can't. They're simply too young and don't understand that their daddy is never coming home again.

A sob escapes my lips, and I throw my hand over my mouth. I close my eyes and count to ten, trying to calm myself down.

They're going to grow up and forget Cain.

The ride to the funeral seems endless. The children are in the backseat bouncing their feet, talking uncontrollably, fussing with one another. I'm sitting in the front passenger seat staring blankly out the window as Pace scolds the kids to behave.

Nothing about today seems right.

This isn't reality.

A panic attack burns straight up from my stomach into my chest leaving me gasping for breath. Hands are on me, a voice surrounds me, but all I can think about is that my love will be lowered into the cold ground, covered with dirt and never able to come home again.

"Paige, Paige," Pace yells, petting me, trying to calm me down. "Breathe, you have to breathe."

The children start to cry, worried why their mommy is acting out of sorts.

My eyes meet Pace's and I start mimicking her breathing. Inhaling and exhaling large amounts of air to calm myself down. After a couple of minutes my body relaxes but the attack has stolen my energy. I put on a smile and turn to the kids.

"Hey, hey now. No crying." I reach back and stroke their little legs. "Mommy is good. Calm down." I do my best to hold myself together so that I can pacify them.

After a few seconds they stop crying but now they're quiet, too quiet. Pace had pulled the car over to deal with my panic attack—now she puts it back in gear and drives the rest of the way to the funeral home. The car is filled with dead air.

Pace parks and we walk into the chapel. I'm running on autopilot as I greet the hundreds of people that show up to give love and support. It's not until we're at the burial site that I snap out of my funk. I get a moment of clarity when the wind blows harder, as if it's whispering words of encouragement. Maybe it's the preacher, I can't tell.

I pull Ivory and Jameson closer to me. I'm unsure if I'm trying to remind them that everything will be okay or if I'm reassuring myself—either way, it comforts me.

When the wind picks up again, a chill runs down my spine. The same chill I used to get every time ... he came around. My reflective sunglasses prevent anyone from seeing my eyes, so I'm able to search the crowd, looking for eyes the same gray as Cain's. Eyes that have haunted me for so long ago.

What would I say if I were to meet Cade again? Nice of you to show up after all this time? Glad you could finally make it to visit? Couldn't you have said goodbye to me before you left so unexpectedly?

Searching the crowd, I don't see him. The man disappeared years ago. Would I know him if I saw him? Would his outer appearance have changed so much that I wouldn't be able to recognize him?

I hug my children even tighter and kiss their heads. As I lift my head, my eyes find a small gap in the crowd and I'm able to see into the tree line. My breathing stops when I spot a shadow standing under a large tree.

"Paige," someone calls.

I narrow my eyes wanting to make out the details of the shadow. It's impossible, I'm unable to make out details so I lean forward a bit only to jump when a hand touches my shoulder.

"Paige, I didn't mean to scare you," the pastor apologizes.

I smile and shake my head. "I'm sorry. I was just lost in my mind."

He gives me an apologetic smile. "I know it's hard but

we're here for you. Please let us know if we can do anything to help you or the children."

When the pastor moves to my in-laws to give them his sympathy, I look around, trying to find the shadow, but it's gone. There's nothing but leaves blowing around on the grass.

Would he have shown up? Would I even recognize him? It's been ten years.

Pace comes over and stands beside me, putting her hand on my arm. "You don't look so well. Why don't I come over and stay a few days? I can help with the kids."

Barely giving her a glance, I nod and say, "I'd like that. Thank you, Pace."

I'm still trying to search through the dispersing crowd for the shadow, even though the funeral home staff have started spreading the flowers over Cain's grave. The act makes my head snap to Cain's resting place until Callie comes over and picks Jameson up. "Do you want me to take the kids so you can rest?" She looks at me with pity.

"Pace is coming home and staying with us for a few days but you're welcome to come over."

I know she won't. She's pregnant with her first child, and her husband, Jack, won't let her out of his sight. I remember Cain being that way. He was always the protector.

Kellie walks up and hugs me from the back. We've been friends since high school and even though we're not as close as Callie and I, we're more than acquaintances. Her son Kip comes running up with his forehead glistening from sweat. I guess the suit he's wearing is a bit more than he's used to.

"Hi Kip. Wow, it's been a while since I've seen you." He smiles and my heart falls straight down to my toes.

"Ms. Paige, I saw you last week."

"Oh," I snap my fingers, acting surprised. "That's right, I forgot."

Kip turns to his mother, "Mom, can I go over to Thomas's? Please," he begs.

He looks so much like Cade, especially with his pleading eyes. Kellie's never said who Kip's father is but it doesn't take a genius to figure that out. Cade disappeared as soon as she found out she was pregnant. That's Cade. Always the first one to get into trouble and the first one to weasel his way out of the consequences.

Cain felt sorry for Kip and did his best to act like a father figure to him. I know inside he did it because he knew Cade was the father.

We exchange a few more words before we make our way to leave.

When Pace pulls the car into my garage, we unload and head into the house. My phone rings as I walk into the kitchen. I don't recognize the area code so I assume it could be a pesky telemarketer.

"Hello," I say skeptically.

There's silence on the phone and goosebumps rise up on my arms. I press the red button, hanging up quickly. My heart races and this time I know it's Cade. My gut screams it.

Why would he wait till Cain died to get back in contact? He's the one who left. No one made him. He choose to walk after everything we'd shared. All the memories of growing up hit me too hard. The boy he used to be is not the man he's become. I remember Cain's words giving me warning of Cade's lifestyle. *"Paige, Cade lives in the darkness outside everything we believe. Life means nothing to him."*

The air in my lungs is coming in large pants. I need to calm down. I can't protect my children's hearts if I can't even protect mine. Callie. She'll know if Cade is back in town.

Soft hands touch my arm, causing me to jump. "Paige.

Are you okay?" Concern is evident on Pace's face.

Instead of answering her, I immediately dial Callie. I have to know if Cade is back. If he's back, it can't be good. He's no good.

I take in the view spread out in the kitchen while I wait for Callie to answer. There are so many dishes of food on the countertop. Large bowls of casseroles line the bar area, and I don't know how we will eat all this before it spoils.

Callie finally answers, "Hey." Her voice is upbeat. If she knew Cade was back in town would she be upbeat?

I don't waste time. I dive in with my question. "Callie, did you see Cade at the funeral today?"

She's silent for a moment.

"No."

One word is all she says. She doesn't say anything else. I wonder if she's waiting on me to say something or just ask questions.

"I didn't see him today. Did you?" But then again, I'm not sure I would recognize him since it's been so long since I saw him last. Just a boy when he left, now he would be a man.

Another moment of silence before she answers, "No."

"Okay. Thanks."

I'm about to hang up the phone when she comments.

She sighs. "He cares, you know."

I answer truthfully, "Callie, I don't understand what happened all those years ago. Do you know why he disappeared? It's like he left and never came back or called."

She doesn't say anything and her silence makes me wonder if she knows. I've never come out and asked. Sure, I've hinted around to get her to tell me. But she's not once given me any idea that she knew anything.

"I've tried to piece things together over the years, but no one has come out and said what actually happened. Cade calls me every year to say happy birthday and I have his number in case I need him."

I believe her. She wouldn't hide anything from me. After we hang up, I walk into my bedroom while Pace plays with the kids in the playroom. The hospital bed is still in the spot against the wall where I pushed it a couple of days ago. It's hard to remember that Cain's not here with us. I lay down on the king-size bed we once shared, spreading my limbs like a starfish and running my hands along the comforter he bought me as a Christmas gift several years ago.

I cry. I cry so hard and so loud that I physically hurt. My eyes, stomach, and head all ache from the pain that is stabbing me in the heart. An agony that no one should have to feel, a torment that robs you of joy. It sits on my chest like a heavy block, suffocating me.

CHAPTER FIVE

Paige

It's been a week since the funeral. I haven't been able to slow down. There are days when I want to lie in bed, throw the cover over my head, and sink into my mattress. The two reasons I can't do that are crawling into my bed to be with me, making sure I'm awake.

"Mommy," Jameson says as he tries to pull the covers down to crawl under and snuggle beside me. Ivory likes to lie on top of the comforter.

"Mommy," Jameson says, a little more forcefully, trying to get my attention.

"Yes, Jameson." I pull the cover back because he's having some trouble with it.

"Let's have brownies for breakfast." He smiles and his dimples are on full display.

I laugh.

He's trouble. Big trouble. I'm going to have my hands full with all that cuteness. Ivory is quiet. She's a thinker. She's four years of age but much older in her maturity level. It leaves me to wonder if her dad's death will affect her in a damaging way.

"How about we have a healthy breakfast?"

He taps his forefinger to his chin and my heart breaks again. Cain does—did that when he was thinking. "Okay, brownies for dessert?" He says in that cute *Elmer Fudd* voice.

I give him a stern look and he blows out air, making his round chubby cheeks squeeze together.

It's times like these that I want to bottle up for my memory bank so I can pull them out later. I reach over and tickle him. I love hearing his full belly laughs. Then we both turn on Ivory, attacking her with our fingers in all her tickle spots.

After breakfast, I get the kids ready for school. We need to get back into a routine. The past few weeks have pulled them away from their friends and learning their lessons. They go to preschool at the primary school where I teach—correction where I used to teach. I left when we realized that Cain wasn't going to get better. I wanted to ensure I soaked up all the time I could spend with him. Looking back, I know I made the right decision. I was able to spend all day every day with him. Some days were tougher than others but I wouldn't have changed it for anything.

When we arrive at the school, I hold their little hands and walk them to their classroom.

"Jameson, are you ready to see your friends?" He smiles up at me and nods.

"Cam says he got a pet dragon!"

Oh great. Now I'm going to be bugged about getting a pet.

Jameson takes off when his door comes in sight.

"No kisses for Mommy?"

No kisses today. He's too excited to be back to his friends.

I look down at Ivory, who's standing in silence.

"Then there were two. You ready to get back to your friends?"

She shrugs her shoulders and looks down the hall to

where her classroom is. "I can stay with you today," she looks up and her eyes hold a heavy burden behind them.

I bend down so that we're face to face, "Baby, you don't worry about Mommy. I'm supposed to take care of you."

"But... you've been sad since Daddy went to sleep."

I take a hold of Ivory's hand and stroke over her knuckles, "I'm going to be okay. We're going to be okay."

Standing back up, I walk her to her door. She goes in but then turns and waves at me. She looks so sad it breaks my heart. Thank goodness her best friend yells her name out as she runs to her, almost tackling Ivory down to the floor. That alone brings a smile to my sweet baby's face. I escape down the hall while she's distracted.

I head to the office to speak to my old boss. I need to go back to work and I'm hoping they still have my old position available. The bills have piled up, and I need something to keep me busy, so I don't have time to feel sorry for myself.

"Sharon, good morning!"

"Good morning, Paige I'm guessing you are dropping off the kids?" Sharon says.

Sharon is an older lady. A little bit older than my mother. She's been working here since her kids were small. Now they are grown and have children of their own.

"Yes, I was hoping Noah was around."

She looks at me, confused. Picking up her pen and notepad, she walks up to the counter to stand in front of me.

"Paige, you don't need to return to work. Take some time off. I'm sure you have things you need to take care of before you try to return." She gives me a pitying look.

The look that everyone gives me. I can't stand it. I want to tell her she shouldn't worry about whether or not I return right away, but I don't. I don't want to hurt her feelings.

Not giving my thoughts away, I continue, "I really need to speak to Noah. Is he around?"

"No, he had a board meeting."

I forgot. They have board meetings every Monday. It's been so long since I've worked here, I've forgotten the weekly schedule.

"Come back Thursday. Nothing is on his schedule. I'll put you down for first thing that morning."

She gives me a smile. I'm angry with her but I accept her offer.

"Great, I will." I tap the countertop. "See you then," I say in my most cheerful voice.

Walking into my house, I yell out, "I'm home, Cain!" I stop in my tracks. All my belongings drop to the floor as the walls start to close in. I drop to my hands and knees, my chest expanding. I crawl to the couch in the living room, hoist myself up and pull my knees to my chest. I sit there and stare at the picture on the opposite wall.

The gray sweater brings out Cain's eyes. His eyes were so bright before he fell ill. I used to lose myself in them.

In the picture, he's standing by Callie and their arms are wrapped around each other. The picture was taken two years ago.

Seems like yesterday.

Thinking back to the days when I hung out all weekend at Callie's, I remember the good times we used to have.

All of us went to school together. Callie and I were in the same grade. Her brothers were older. Cain was always the good brother and son, while Cade was always in trouble. He wasn't the best student or the best son, but his parents loved him just as much as their other children. Shortly after I turned eighteen, Cade disappeared. We never saw him again.

I tried to get Cain to find him. To reach out to him. He would tell me to drop it. Eventually, I did. I never mentioned it again. I grew tired of trying to bring all three of them back together again. Now I know that Callie has stayed in touch with him. This brings me some relief that he wasn't alone and cut off from his family.

At some point, I straightened out to lay on the couch, and I've been lying here in the same spot all day, not bothering to get up to wash dishes, do laundry or clean the house. Just staring into space, thinking that all this is a dream and that I will wake up any moment and Cain will be in the next room. Rolling to my side, I see the clock above the fireplace and notice it's time for me to go pick up the kids.

I pull myself off the plush sofa cushion, grab my purse, and head out into the garage. I'm not paying too much attention to where I'm going when I run into Cain's set of golf clubs that were leaning against an inconvenient spot against the wall. They fall, but not before one of them clocks me in the eye.

"Son of a bitch!" I yell out.

I'm so angry. I open the garage door and throw the clubs one by one into the yard, cursing. "Stupid, fucking clubs. Can you not pick up your shit, Cain?"

When I throw the last one, I'm left standing, looking at a very expensive set of golf clubs scattered on my front lawn. I scream. Trying to push out all the frustration that's pent up in my body. Tears leave the corners of my eyes, and I close my hands over my face as I drop onto the paved driveway.

My neighbor, Jimmy, comes over and asks me questions but I'm too angry to answer. I'm too agitated to care. I sit down with my head low, irritated that Cain didn't move those clubs when I asked him to do it so long ago. I told him over and over to put them in a better place. Then I'm angry at myself for not moving them when I had noticed he didn't. Finally, coming to my senses, I realize it doesn't matter. The golf clubs are not the issue. It's me.

"Paige," Jimmy shakes me.

Damp tears cover my cheeks and I swipe them away. "Hey," I do my best to sound like I haven't totally lost my mind.

"Let me help you." Jimmy holds his hand out.

I gladly take it. He helps pull me up.

"I …" I don't even know how to explain what happened.

He puts his hand on my shoulder. "Don't worry about it," Jimmy says. "When I lost my wife, I threw everything out of the freezer. She never put a twist tie on anything after opening it. I was reaching in the freezer to grab a bag of frozen peas. The bag opened as I lifted it and the damn things went everywhere. I went into a rage and emptied the whole freezer." He chuckles. "I'm guessing something like that went wrong here." He looks at the lawn.

I give a sad smile and nod. "I bumped into them. I used to ask him to put them in the corner of the garage, so they weren't in the way. Silly, I know."

He squeezes my shoulder. "Sometimes we need people to talk things out. You know my group for widows helped me a great deal. Come on, let's get these high priced metal sticks out of the yard."

We pick up the clubs in silence and put them in the garage in a place where they should be out of the way.

Jimmy says goodbye and tells me to call him if I need anything. He's a pleasant man in his sixties. He married his high school sweetheart and lost her to a heart attack last year around the time we discovered Cain's illness. He's been a godsend the past year. The best handy man to have around. He's fixed and corrected more stuff while Cain was ill than Cain had in all the years we were married.

CHAPTER SIX

Paige

It's been a week since my breakdown, and I'm sitting outside watching the kids play. We live in the country, just outside of the small community I grew up in. My parents are both retired and now live primarily in Florida at their condo. My sister stays in the family home while she attends the nearby college.

This morning the kids complained when I wanted to do nothing but lay on the couch. But laying around, caught up in my feelings about living my life without Cain, is something I'm unable to do with two small children. They keep me going. I want to be grateful for the distraction but there's a side of me that is so depressed about him not being here—even if the last few months he was sleeping ninety percent of the day. At least he was still here.

Stretched out in a lounge chair on the deck, I watch the children run around in the backyard. I close my eyes as I inhale the fresh air. Behind my closed eyelids, I feel a shadow block the light; opening them, I adjust my eyes when the sunlight momentarily blinds me. Pace stands over me with a smile. Since Cain's death, we've swapped roles, and she's taken the big sister role, ensuring I'm okay.

"Hey, Sunshine," Pace says with a perky voice.

The last thing I feel like is sunshine.

"Have a seat," I point to the lounge chair close to me.

Pace pulls the chair closer and stretches out on it.

"Yesterday, I saw Katie Gunn," she comments.

"Katie Gunn?" Why does that name sound familiar?

"You remember Katie John-Gunn. She went to school with you."

I think about it, "Oh yeah. I remember now. She was elected Most Likely to Succeed."

"I guess that's true... you forget that I'm five years younger than you."

"That's because you weren't planned," I smile over at her. "They got it right the first time."

She rolls her eyes at me.

"Any who... her husband was killed six months ago. She attends a widows' group every two weeks. Katie said if it weren't for the group, she wouldn't be able to get out of bed in the morning. I told her about Cain, and she gave me the information to pass along to you." Pace reaches into her pocket and hands me a piece of folded up paper.

I'm hesitant to take it but I do. I open it and look at the name and number written on the paper.

"Katie said for you to call her. She wanted to talk to you. Said that if she just wrote the next meeting location, she knew you would make excuses not to come."

"I don't need to go. I'm fine..." I trail off into silence.

"You're not fine, Paige. I've watched you. When you think no one is watching, your happy front drops and your face tells how unsteady you are. Give Katie a call. It may help more than you realize," she pleads.

She reaches over and places her hand on mine, trying to comfort me.

I give her a knowing smile. What would I do without her?

Our conversation is stopped when Ivory spots Pace. Ivory yells out in excitement and starts running toward us, and not a second later Jameson screams out too, trailing behind his sister.

Weeks later I am still trying to fool everyone into believing I'm okay but the sad part is I've stopped believing it myself. I've been running on fumes, but now I feel like I'm about to completely run out of energy. Sleepless nights have me awake, rehashing what I could have done differently in the past. My depression has hit an all-time low and I know without a doubt I've got to do something.

After I drop the kids off, I sit in my car in the school parking lot and dial Katie's number.

"You've reached Katie. I'm unavailable but leave your name and number and I'll get back with you." *Beep.*

"Katie, this is Paige Staton… I wanted…" *Why is this so hard? Just rip the bandage off.* "I wanted to see about the meetings Pace was telling me about. Just give me a call back. This is my cell number. Thanks." *Click.*

I'm still sitting in my car when minutes later, she returns my call.

"Hi Paige."

"Hey, how are you?"

"I'm good, just busy with work. I'm so glad you reached out. I told Pace I wasn't going to call you but I came close. How have you been?"

I close my eyes and take a large breath. I haven't really told anyone the truth about how I've been feeling or been functioning.

"I take it from your silence you haven't been doing so

great," Katie comments.

"Not so great. I've been holding it together, but barely. I wanted to speak to you about going to one of the grief support meetings Pace was telling me about."

"After I buried Don, I couldn't raise my head off the pillow. I laid in bed not even wanting to get back to life. He was my everything. The one person I never thought anything would happen to. But then there was the motorcycle wreck and..." She breaths out heavily. "I still have hard times but it's gotten better. The support group helps. They listen when I talk about my bad days. They listen to my good days too, but most of all they care..."

Maybe talking to strangers is exactly what I need after all.

Katie says my name loudly, pulling me out of my thoughts.

"Paige! Are you there?"

"Yes. I... sorry, I got lost in my head."

"It's fine. You have a lot on your mind."

Katie goes on letting me know when the next meeting is and gives me an address. I quickly write it down and agree to meet her there.

I start the car and drive home on autopilot. The conversation with Katie plays in my mind on the ride back to my house. How she lost her husband in a split moment and didn't get to say good-bye. Having someone walk out the door and never to come back through it must be... devastating.

The next week flies by and before I know it, it's time for the meeting. I've been on the fence about it all week. Staring at myself in the mirror, I try to decide if I really need this. Can I tell these strangers how I'm truly feeling? The loss that I feel at no longer having my husband with me. With shaky hands I pick up my phone.

I can't, I just can't meet people and tell them all about Cain's illness and how hard it was to watch him get weaker and weaker. They won't understand.

I'm about to send Katie a text when my phone rings in my hand.

"I can feel it from here. You're changing your mind about coming," Katie says even before I can say hello.

"How did you know that?"

"I did the same thing on my first meeting. You don't think people will know what you went through and you don't want people to think you're weak. You're not, you know."

"I'm not what?" I ask, curious as to what she thinks.

"Weak… You're not weak just because you share your feelings. It's more," she pauses, "of a strengthening process. Kind of like you letting go of the old you and giving the new you a way to become stronger. Together we strengthen each other. You'll see. Do you want me to pick you up?"

"That's not necessary I can find it."

"It's not about finding it. I don't want you to get cold feet and not come. I promise you the group won't judge you if you break down. They won't judge you when you get angry over things you're left to deal with. They're here to listen and support you on the path you're left to take."

I know she's right. I can do this.

CHAPTER SEVEN

Cade

The warm water flowing over my bloody hands sends a stream of red down the drain. My life sure didn't turn out like I thought it would. It's not the life I wanted. It's all because of one man and now that he's gone there's nothing standing in my way to having what I've always wanted. What has always been mine.

I close my eyes and picture her soft features while Bradford Martin's loud whimpers echo behind me. I do my best to block the sound out as I continue to think about her. The one woman I've waited far too long to have. I'm ready to take what should have been mine but I know she's not ready, not yet. I need to be patient. Allow her to mourn the death of her beloved husband. Beloved. I want to laugh at the thought of Cain ever loving anyone more than himself. I scrub my hands harder as I relive the past.

The memories of her smile, so sweet, so genuine, send a warm shot to my icy heart. Then I remember how Cain stole her from me and my blood begins to burn through my veins like lava.

For so long I've wanted to bury him for blackmailing me,

for forcing me to leave, for the mocking smirk on his stupid face that night.

Cain was ready for me, slouched against the wall, his hands in his jeans pockets, waiting for me when I got back to the dorm.

"Did you hear about Mitch's dad? It looks like a car accident." Cain's voice is laced with menace as he narrows his eyes and, once again, the slits remind me of the snake he really is.

I play the innocent card while Cain throws his joker at me, a painful reminder that he will always be considered the golden boy.

"No?" The single word I utter comes out as a deadly question.

I stand my ground, though, determined to not give myself away—only to fail with his next words.

"I'm thinking you already knew his dad was dead." He cocks his head. "Hmm... wonder how my sweet Paige would see you if she knew?"

I grit my teeth. He knows my weakness and uses it against me, "She's not yours," I state, balling my fist up.

"Oh but she wants to be and I'm guessing when she finds out that you murdered Mitch's dad you'll never have a chance with her—not that you had one in the first place," he taunts.

"Why do you think I knew?"

He pulls his right hand from his pocket and holds up a playing card. It's my lucky Ace. Dad gave it to me when he taught me how to play poker. He wrote on it, "To my lucky Ace" because I always won when I played with him and his friends. He never had a gambling problem, he just liked to play for fun. But I took pleasure in bleeding his and his friends' wallets dry.

I reach for my back pocket. Shit, it's not there. I know I stuffed it in there before I went out tonight, but it must have slid out somehow during the commotion.

"To my lucky Ace... so sweet." He forms his lips into a pout.

"How did you get that?"

"Oh, I have friends who happened to see it at a certain crash site. A crash site they're pretty sure was set up to look like an accident but

really... wasn't." He lifts an eyebrow.

Crap. I know it was Jordy. He's a rookie cop and one of Cain's close friends.

"What do you want?" My voice is strained. I don't even recognize it.

"What do I want?" He pretends to look up at the ceiling thinking, tapping his index finger to his chin. When he looks back at me his eyes are ablaze. "I want you to leave and never come back."

My family thinks I left that night. I called my parents and told them I was done with college, that it wasn't for me. That I wanted to work with a friend who had opened a business across the country. They weren't happy but there wasn't anything they could do, I was of legal age, and I knew if they found out what I had done, it would have destroyed them and a lot of other people, too.

Did I feel remorse for killing Mitch's dad? No way in hell. He had it coming and, if you think about it, he got off easy — easier than his victims. He raped Mitch when he was a boy. Then used Mitch to lure other young boys in. I didn't find out until it was too late.

When I found Mitch, he was holding a letter explaining everything in detail. How he was raped at seven years old.

Mitch had thought that college was his only way out. He graduated from high school at the top of his class, and received a scholarship, but two hundred miles away from home still couldn't get him away from his dad.

The day he killed himself his dad had called telling him he needed him to come home to help him with his plans of abusing a neighborhood boy—and if he didn't, he would turn Mitch in to the police and tell them Mitch that had raped all those boys.

Fear for his life, and for the other lives that had and would be affected, placed a heavy burden on him. The only way he saw out was to seek a resolution that brought his life to an end.

But there was no way Cain would understand that I wanted justice for my friend. The only way justice could be served. A life for a life. Mitch's dad's life for the life he took from Mitch.

Cain was only interested in getting me out of the picture so that he could continue spreading his pack of lies to everyone. So, I did what seemed best at the time and left. Very early the next morning.

What he had over me then would have destroyed what I was working toward. The only girl I'd ever really wanted... Paige.

Cain had always wanted what I had or what I wanted. He was a pro at setting me up to take the fall for his evil actions.

I clench my fist as I remember giving in and choosing to be the person everyone perceived me to be. In that very moment I gave Cain the power to banish me from the most precious gift I could have ever received. To have a life with Paige. Instead, he took it from me.

When Bradford cries out again, I shake away these unwanted memories. But as much as I want to forget them, forget the past, they are branded into my memory, as permanent as if they were locked tight in a vault with a galvanized steel chain holding them in place. There just seems to be no getting rid of them.

Alcohol and drugs don't erase the memory of Paige's face, the smell of her hair, or how soft her skin is. I put my hand up to my chest, rubbing it. The same piercing chest pain occurs every time I remember the night I spent with her.

I can feel myself getting more agitated and so I close my eyes and inhale the stench of Bradford's blood and piss, trying to ground myself in this moment. It's my only tranquility. Focusing on the pain of others has been my way of coping with the burning pain of losing Paige. It's the only way to dull it.

I turn off the faucet, dry my hands on a towel, and lift my gaze to the broken mirror above the sink.

My eyes meet Bradford's in the cracked glass. His face is a mess—I've already given him a good working over, but he has no idea what's coming.

Keeping eye contact, I curl my lips up on one side, relishing the fear that radiates off him. He widens his bloodshot eyes knowing that my fun has just started.

A man on his knees, crying, is not a good look but he should have thought about that before he put his hands on an eight-year-old boy.

"Bradford, Bradford," I sing.

I take in his physique as I make my way back over, circling him. He's a skinny mother fucker. His hair is longer on top with the sides cut short. His broken boney fingers bleed from the wounds caused by the steel pipe I used to crush them. I shudder when I think about those long boney fingers touching a small, innocent boy.

"Drop your pants, Bradford."

His whole body shakes but he doesn't move. He's still looking at me with wide eyes, using them to silently beg for forgiveness. He won't find it here. No adult has the right to touch an innocent child.

"You can take them off or I can cut them off." I shrug my shoulder. "Either way works for me."

"Are you going to tell her?" Dillion asks.

I lift my glass and the ice clinks against the crystal. Water is my designated drink. I no longer drink alcohol. It doesn't numb the pain of the past and it doesn't stop the memories from resurfacing. So I choose to stay sober, especially since it gives me the most control over the memories that plague me.

When I quit college, disappearing from my family and friends virtually without a trace, drugs and alcohol became an everyday habit I couldn't survive without. I finally sobered my ass up when I'd eventually had enough of waking up and not remembering what had happened to me for days. I can remember the last time I was high. I woke up in an abandoned warehouse laying on a lice-infested mattress with a needle in my arm.

I shake my head at the memory, as I've done countless times before. A higher power must have shown me grace that day and put a plan for my redemption in place. I saved a man's life in an alley that day—Dillion. He's become my friend and mentor. He helped me discover my talent for finding people who don't want to be found.

"I...I'm not sure," I tell him honestly.

"She has a right to know," he continues.

My eyes are set on the glass in front of me. "If I tell her of her husband's secret life, won't she hate me?"

He shrugs a shoulder. Dillion is the only person that knows what happened between me and Cain.

"Or if I tell her and she doesn't believe me, will she hate me even more?"

Dillion opens his mouth but closes it, thinking for a moment before he speaks.

"Either way she's going to hate you. I imagine finding out those things after you buried someone would make you bitter. Hell, I'd be so bitter I'd go and set their grave on fire."

He would probably burn down the whole cemetery. Dillion leaves no stone unturned when he's pissed.

"You're right. That's why I have a plan."

I stand and throw a hundred dollar bill on the bar. "Get

home safely." Then I turn and leave, already making plans
for my trip.

When I pull up to the school yard, it's easy to identify
Ivory. She has the exact same features as her mom—it's like
she's Paige's mini-me.

She's surrounded by a few other small children. One of
the boys pushes Ivory down and the other kids laugh. I look
around, wondering where their teacher is. It doesn't take
long to spot her flaming red hair. She's sitting with other
teachers. None of them are paying attention to the children
that are playing in the yard. Instead, they're either on their
phones or talking among themselves.

I get out of my car, shut the door, walk over to the fence
and holler out to the boy. "You," I yell, pointing to the dark-
haired boy. His eyes almost bug out when he spots me.

At his young age, I know what he sees. A six-foot four
man wearing nothing but black—black boots, black pants,
and black tee, and any visible skin covered in tattoos. He's
scared. He should be.

"Apologize to her," I bark out.

The boy is frozen in place, still staring at me.

I lower my voice, "If you don't apologize, I'll come to your
house tonight and make your parents regret the day they
had you."

He swallows. The wheels are finally starting to turn in
his little brain.

"I'm sorry," he says to Ivory. Then in a flash, he darts off
like a scared little rabbit.

Ivory's eyes pull away from the back of the young boy
and she turns her head to look at me. Slowly she trails her
eyes over the body art that covers my neck, hands, and

exposed arms. She studies it, trying to read the story there, and I stand still for her scrutiny. When she raises her eyes, they grow bigger as they rest on my face. It's as if I can see inside of her small mind and all the questions she's asking herself. Who is he? Why does he look...

"Who are you?" her sweet voice asks, cutting off my thoughts.

I can tell she's not afraid of me. She's more curious. She gets up and dusts herself off as she walks over to the fence and stares up at me.

"You look like..."

"Ivory!" Her teacher rushes over to her and pulls her back by her shoulders. She ushers Ivory away before I get a chance to answer her question. "We don't talk to strangers," the teacher whispers a little loudly.

"But he's..." Ivory peers back at me over her shoulder.

"Don't argue, Ivory," her teacher's voice is laced with sternness.

I grit my teeth to keep from lashing out. The teacher is clearly trying to keep Ivory safe, but I'm not happy with the tone she used.

"But..." Ivory's shoulders slump while the teacher pushes her toward the small school building's double doors.

I stay planted to the same spot and watch them walk off, hoping for one more glance back from Ivory. The little girl who already has a piece of my heart.

When they've entered the building and I can no longer see their shadows. I walk away feeling a little bit more determined to make her a part of my everyday life.

CHAPTER EIGHT

Paige

Six Months Later

The desktop calendar stares at me, haunting me with the memories. I buried Cain six months to this day. Only two things have changed in the short amount of time that has passed. My mental breakdowns have become less frequent in the past six months and I accepted a new position as a sixth grade teacher at the middle school. I could have had my old position back, but I thought it would be a good change for me and it's proven to be.

A new classroom in a different school building has given me a fresh beginning. Of course there are more challenges in teaching sixth graders but at least most of the children are still sweet at that age.

What I miss most about my old school is not being able to peek in on Jameson and Ivory throughout the day. But the primary and middle school buildings are close to each other so it doesn't take long for me to get there to pick them up after the dismissal bell rings.

Today is Saturday and I'm going through the endless stack of bills piled high in front of me. I've looked through each bill and now it's time to decide who gets paid and how much this month. We incurred so much debt from all the care Cain needed. I applied for financial aid on the ones I could. Some were knocked out but there's still a staggering amount to be paid off.

The experimental treatments we participated in were not covered by insurance and those bills are the largest. We were hopeful those treatments would work, only to be disappointed when they didn't. Just the prescriptions required by those new treatments cost enough to buy a small country.

Life insurance wasn't a thought before Cain was diagnosed with cancer. Then afterwards, well, we couldn't get insurance because of preexisting conditions. The small policy he had through the school wasn't paid out because he had to quit working due to his health.

When you're young things like cancer don't sneak into your mind and when you hear that word you sure as hell don't think it's going to happen to you. I throw the bill I'm holding down onto the table. Running the tips of my fingers over my forehead, I push them into my hair, grab the thick strands by the roots, and tug at them. If it wasn't for my children, I would fall apart. They're the reason I get up everyday, head to work, and make it till bedtime. Most nights I cry myself to sleep.

I need a break from looking at these.

When I stand, I make my way into the walk-in closet I once shared with Cain. I haven't done anything with his clothes yet—they all still hang right next to mine. Spotting Cain's black bomber jacket, I gather it up in my arms and hug it close to my chest. I bought the jacket for his birthday a few years ago. I can still picture his face when he opened the large box and pulled it out. A smile tugs at my lips when I remember how excited he was, how proud he was when he pulled it out. He wore the jacket even when it wasn't cold enough. I bury my nose into the material. His scent still lingers on the collar.

God, I miss him.

Tears escape the corners of my eyes and soak into the jacket's fabric. I slide my hands down the jacket remembering how it felt when Cain's body filled it out. The fingers on my left hand snag on a pocket opening and something falls out and hits the floor with a soft thump.

I sniff, trying to stop my nose from running. Wiping my eyes with the back of my hand, I eye the folded piece of notebook paper that just fell to the floor. I bend and pick it up, carrying it and the jacket with me as I sit on the bed. I unfold the paper wondering if Cain had left a final goodbye.

My heart drops when I notice the letter isn't addressed to me. It's addressed to a person named—Kay, and it's alarming.

Kay,

I need more time to tell Paige. I don't want to hurt her. I want to make sure there's nothing in the way that can come between us when I tell her. My health is a concern, and I'm growing weaker each day. Just know that I'll always love …

The letter ends. Not saying if he'll always love me or … her. I feel sick, and rush to the adjacent bathroom. I drop to my knees and every ounce in my stomach comes back up in a rush. It doesn't stop until I'm dry heaving.

A few seconds later I reach up to grab the hand towel hanging on the rack above the commode. I use it to wipe my eyes and mouth and then slump back to the floor.

I slide backwards to prop myself up against the wall. My hands tremble, and I realize I am still clutching the unfinished letter.

I glance down at it again and notice the date at the top— three months after we found out he had cancer. A time when shock was still settling into our minds, while we were still wondering why cancer had happened to Cain.

My mind wanders back in time to the days before his cancer, when I thought Cain was acting weird. The late night runs he would take. He told me he needed to clear his head, release the stress, of all the extra circular activities he was volunteering for at the school. I believed him.

I knew he had taken on too much, but I would not have ever thought there was a possibility he was having an affair. It never occurred to me. I thought we were happy. I thought we had it all. Our beautiful children, the house we worked so hard on to restore, and a love that could weather the toughest times. What a naïve fool I was.

I throw the towel against the wall screaming out my frustrations.

Who else knew of his affair? Had people been talking about it behind my back? Why didn't I see it? I thought he was happy. I thought we were happy. How could I have been so blind? Was he planning on divorcing me?

My mind is swirling with different scenarios. I feel betrayed. I took care of him. I loved him. And *this* is the thanks I get? A letter confessing his undying love for another woman.

My blood is rushing through my body, roaring in my ears. I'm growing more enraged the longer I think about how I cared for him, and he kept this secret from me.

I hear a commotion in the house, and I quickly re-fold the paper and stuff it in my pocket. Swiftly coming up to stand, I take in my complexion in the mirror. My shoulders slump, and I feel the same vulnerability I felt when Cain passed. I feel like all the work I've put in these past six months to adjust to this new normal has come undone. Now, instead of grief, the feeling of betrayal by the one person who was supposed to love me till death is strongest. The problem is, I loved him till death, and now I'm left to deal with this. All the bills, the self-doubt, and now this new feeling that I meant nothing to him.

The sound of small feet running in the house grows louder.

"Mommy," Jameson yells.

I swipe under my eyes trying to wipe away the smears of mascara.

No sooner have I cleared under my eyes, then my beautiful children run into me, almost knocking me down. Ivory hugs my left leg while Jameson is on my right.

"Did you have a good time at the museum?" I ask the children.

Their tiny faces show the evidence that they had a great time. There's chocolate around their cute little mouths. I lick my finger and bring it close to Jameson's mouth to wipe away the stain.

"No Mommy! Gross," he says as he jerks out of my reach.

I laugh at his cuteness.

"We had a great time," Pace says as she comes into the bedroom. "The kiddos played all day. I didn't even hear any bickering between them."

I raise my eyebrows, "What? You weren't fussing?"

"No, we played with Cade," Jameson remarks.

The hairs on the back of my neck and on my arms stand up. I slowly raise my eyes until they collide with Pace's.

"What?" I whisper.

The children look at me, waiting to see if I react further. I crouch down to their eye level and grab hold of Jameson's shoulders.

"Did you say you played with Cade?"

Jameson nods.

"Yes," Ivory confirms.

I close my mouth to still my breathing.

It's not the same Cade... surely, it's not.

Maybe, they met a child named Cade. I could be just overreacting. Cade is a grown man. He wouldn't be in a children's museum.

Then why is my heart pounding so loud that my neighbor could probably hear it?

I stand up, turn to the sink and grip the edges of the counter so hard I'm surprised it doesn't crack.

A panic attack is starting to creep up on me and I have to grab the edges of the counter. Today's been too much. First the bills with their unpayable balances, second the unexpected letter, and lastly hearing the name *Cade.*

The following week, I sit in my grief support group's circle, where we speak of our feelings and try to help ourselves heal from the hurt of losing our loved ones.

The plastic chairs are hard—much like how my heart has grown since I found Cain's letter. I haven't felt any better than the day I found the letter.

"Paige." Someone calls my name.

I'm so lost in thoughts of this new hurt that I feel I haven't paid any attention to what each member of the support group has said.

"Paige, would you like to share anything?" the counselor asks.

I look at Katie. I haven't told her.

I take a moment, letting my eyes roam around the group. Praying their eyes won't hold any judgment once I speak of the letter.

"Hi, I'm Paige Staton." I start the same each time it's my turn to speak.

Everyone has a style they start off with. Mine is to tell my name and about Cain's illness.

I shift in my chair, the anguish building up, making my seat uncomfortable. My leg bounces, and I'm apprehensive about telling my story.

Katie's hand touches mine. I lay my second hand on top of hers. The gesture helps calm my nerves. I give her a faint smile, silently thanking her.

"Last week, I was in my closet holding onto Cain's favorite coat. I know it sounds strange." I shake my head. "I wanted to hold him. I wanted to be close to him," I close my mouth, unsure if telling them will make me feel better.

Tears spill out, blurring my vision and trickling down my checks. I wipe them away because what I found doesn't deserve my tears. The sight of the circle of caring faces surrounding me fuels my fire. These are not tears for the once great love I thought I had lost. These are tears of anger. I'm angry because I thought we had something most couples never have, a timeless love.

Stupid me.

A burst of laughter escapes and I quickly cover my mouth. The expressions on the faces of my fellow group members don't change and I can't help it when another laugh escapes me. This time it doesn't just escape, it releases from my belly. I'm freaking delusional with laughter.

What is happening to me?

Crazy? I must be going insane.

When the laughter stops, I feel drained of energy. Julia, who is our counselor, speaks.

"Paige, you're welcome to continue."

I want nothing more than to vanish on the spot, but I reply in a small voice. "Thank you."

A moment of doubt passes in my mind about whether I should finish the story, but I pull the strength up from somewhere deep inside me.

Everyone sits in their seats, their nonjudgment gazes focused on me, waiting for what I will say or do next. Suddenly, I feel exposed—as if I'm standing in front of a firing squad naked.

Pulling the folded up paper from my pants pocket, I hold it up for everyone to see.

"I found this in a pocket of one of Cain's coats last week," I say bitterly. "I was holding his favorite jacket, you know," I laugh. "So, I could feel close to him," another laugh bubbles up. "Yeah, well I knocked this letter out of his pocket and when I read it… let's just say I feel like a fool. Would you like me to read it to you?" I ask, letting my anger peak. Not waiting for anyone to reply, I unfold the paper not so gracefully, then read it out loud.

When I'm finished, I look around at the people I've come to know over the past few months. There's still no judgement in their eyes, but I can feel their pity. I mentally kick myself. *Why did I have to tell them? Why?*

No one utters a word.

CHAPTER NINE

Cade

The primary school beckons to me like the bright lamp in a lighthouse, guiding me home from the stormy seas. It has led me from the fatal shoals I've endured during my time away, back to the life I want. The life I desire to have with Paige. The life Cain took away from me.

Bitter is how I imagined I would feel when I finally met Cain's children, but I was wrong. It's not bitterness that I feel, it's envy. Since I first saw Ivory here, when she was pushed down by that bully, I've tied up some loose ends with Dillion, sold most of my possessions and moved myself back to this town. It took a few months to get everything in order, and to smooth things over with Dillion—who is not happy about this change, but now I've found myself every afternoon this week parked outside the primary school. Then, as if I'm on autopilot, I'm out of my car and leaning against the fence, my gaze seeking the tiny blonde to watch her play with her school mates.

Being here and hoping to talk to Ivory is a dangerous game I'm playing, but I can't help myself. I want to get to know Paige's children, become a part of their everyday life.

I'm in luck today, as Ivory walks toward me. I wonder if she remembers me from my first visit?

"Do you like my dress?" Ivory asks.

"It's very pink and pretty," I tell her honestly.

"Thank you. My mom let me pick it out. She says I can pick out my own clothes now." I smile as I listen to her go on and on. "I'm a big girl. My mom tells me I'm growing up too fast."

"You do look taller than yesterday," I tease her.

Ivory gives me an adorable expression.

"I haven't grown any since yesterday silly. My daddy used to measure my height on my door but..." She looks down at her feet before she kicks the dirt. "He's not coming back."

I could ask her where's he at, but I already know the answer. If this was anyone else talking, I would be a dick and tell them I think he was a piece of shit, but I won't do that to a little girl. I won't ruin her happy memories of him. She needs to hold on to them for as long as she can.

"I know that wherever he's at, he's thinking about you."

"Ivory!" The teacher yells from across the playground. She starts running toward us, calling out again. "Ivory, get away from that stranger." The teacher comes up and grabs Ivory by the shoulders, turning her to face the opposite direction of me. "Go stand by our color block, we're going back inside."

Once Ivory is out of hearing range, her teacher snaps around to face me.

"I don't know who you are, but if I see you around the play yard again, I'm calling the police." Without another word she storms off, her fast pace kicking up the gravel.

It's my turn to call out to the teacher.

"Ms. Lambert." She stops in her tracks when it registers that I know her name. She doesn't turn back to me she just stands still. "We seem to be new neighbors. You live on Sycamore Street, right?"

Ms. Lambert's back looks like a rod was threaded through her vertebrae. I can sense her fear, but she doesn't say anything. She doesn't turn around. Instead, she squares her shoulders and walks over to Ivory, calling out for the children to gather up. Her eyes dart over to where I'm standing but she quickly diverts them.

When the students march off, I remain in the same spot. My eyes follow Ivory as she turns back to wave goodbye, then she steps inside. When the last student disappears, I push off the chain link fence and head to my car. My black Porsche is parked down the street just enough to be discreet but still allow me to have a bird's eye view of the school's parking lot where Paige parks every afternoon.

I'm not sitting there long when the dismissal bell rings for school and a few minutes later Paige arrives and parks her white SUV.

She still steals my breath. Her dark hair whips around in the wind, and so does the skirt of the long floral dress she has on. It hugs her waist but hides just enough of her beautiful legs so as to not give any hint as to how sexy she is.

This brief moment of seeing her is not enough. I decide to wait till she comes back out to get one more look at her, Jameson and Ivory before I leave. The suspense of having to wait till tomorrow to see her again claws at my skin like a bearcat.

Time slowly creeps by as I wait for Paige to emerge with the kids. She's taking longer than normal. A restless feeling slowly consumes me as I realize that the teacher is probably filling Paige's ears up with stories of me.

Paige finally comes out with Jameson on her hip and a death grip on Ivory's hand. She looks around like a scared rabbit and almost runs to her car. Quickly putting the kids into their seats, she hurries over to the driver's side.

My pocket vibrates and I pull my phone out. Dillion's name pops up on my screen.

"Dillion."

"Are you still stalking her?"

"Stalking who?"

He laughs. "You know who. Don't take me for a fool. I know what you've been doing each day."

"Who's stalking who then?"

"It's my job to keep up with you. I need to make sure you're not getting into any shit you shouldn't be."

"Hmm… did you call me for a reason or are you calling me to bust my balls?"

"Both." He laughs.

"Okay… now that you've given me shit tell me what you're really calling about."

He's silent for a moment.

"We've lost him."

"When?" I quiz.

"Just now." He pauses a beat. "I followed him to California but lost him at the airport. He's traveling with his wife. They apparently booked a flight under another name. I had no idea they had plans to leave since he's originally from Santa Monica. I need you to meet me in Mexico. I've got a hunch he's headed there. I'm going to need your help."

My lungs deflate. Me leaving here wasn't ever in my plans. I'm ready to settle down, leave behind this life of taking the trash out. I've been thinking about going legit, opening up my own private investigating business. Cain's gone now and buried with him are the secrets of the past. I just need to give Paige a little more space. Callie told me Paige goes to a grief support group—I need to let the group help her heal and become stronger. So she'll be ready to begin a future with me.

"Send me all the details and I'll catch the next flight out, but right now I need to pay a visit to an old rival."

I end the call and push the start button on my car. Shifting the car into gear, I make my way to the other side of town.

Twenty minutes later, I park my car in front of the iron gate. It's too quiet, not a living soul in sight. All that stands here are stones with the names and dates of the deceased.

A chill runs through me as I weave through the graves, trying not to step on the dead. My feet stop in front of a marble stone: Cain Staton, loving husband and father.

Loving husband, if only they knew.

I lean against the large oak that overshadows Cain's grave.

"Nice tree, Cain. I can see why she buried you in this spot. I wonder if the shadow of the tree helps chill the heat in the pits of hell. Does it?" I kick at the base of his marker. "Does she know? Does she know that you pushed me away from my family... from her?" I run my hand through my short hair. "But there's one thing I've always had you couldn't take. One thing that's kept me going. The only thing that's saved my sanity. And that's knowing I," I thump my chest, "was her first." I go silent for a moment, while the wind rustles the leaves and whistles around the headstones, before I continue. "Does she know your secret?"

There's a gasp from behind me and it makes me jump around. A blue hood is pulled over a small figure concealing the person's identity. They continue to walk briskly in the direction of the parking lot. I strain to look past them and see a white SUV parked one space over from my car.

Shit! It's Paige.

"Paige!" I scream her name and start after her.

She turns back to look at me before she takes off running to her vehicle. I lengthen my stride but she makes it to her SUV before I can get to her. Jumping in, she cranks it then throws it into reverse.

Running beside the SUV, I try to open the door only to find it's locked.

"Paige," I beat on the window. "Paige! Please stop!"

A brief moment passes before she turns to look me in the eye. Pain fills her eyes, pain that I've caused her.

I didn't want her to find out like this, how it was me instead of Cain that night at her birthday party. The night I took her virginity. I knew she was expecting Cain but with Cain's threat from earlier that day, I wanted one night, one moment in time to hold on to... forever.

Paige throws the car into drive, speeding out of the parking lot and down the gravel drive.

I stand in the middle of the parking lot, raking my hands through my hair, wishing I could go back to my teenage years. So, I could change the day Cain took control of my life. The emptiness that I've felt since that day.

Buzz, buzz.

My phone vibrates with a call. Crap. Dillion is calling again.

"Yeah."

"I've got you a flight booked, and you need to be ready to leave in two hours. Go home, pack everything. We may be gone for some time."

I huff, not wanting to leave things with Paige in this manner.

"I don't know, Dillion. I've got stuff to take care of here." I say quietly.

"Come on, man. Let's take care of this job. We've already gotten paid half. Once we finish this one, if you still want to split, then that's fine. But be careful. If you're doing this for a woman make sure she's a sure thing before you give up everything."

I know he's right. I need to make sure she loves me before I change my whole life.

"Alright. I'm headed home to grab a bag. Email me the flight details."

When we hang up, I take one more look down the road, wishing I could go after her.

CHAPTER TEN

Paige

I'm in no condition to drive—a thousand horses could be galloping on my chest and it wouldn't hurt any worse than hearing Cade's words. But no sooner have I dragged my mind back to the road, then it takes off again.

Does she know your secret?

The ache that is consuming me hardens my heart. What is his secret? What did Cain feel the need to hide from me? Was it his affair with Kay? But how would Cade know about that?

My emotions are all over the place—sad, angry, upset over this secret. When I finally pull into my driveway I don't bother parking the car in the garage.

"You weren't gone long," Pace greets me.

I don't respond. Instead, I walk past her and go straight to the walk-in closet in bedroom. I look at Cain's side and start grabbing boxes, suitcases, his pants and jackets—anything with pockets or that I think something might be hidden in, and toss it all on the floor.

"Paige, what are you doing? What's wrong?" Pace asks from the closet doorway, panic in her voice.

I let go of the shoe box in my hand, and it falls to the floor.

"Cade was at the cemetery." Pace's face falls. "I walked up behind him, not realizing it was him until I was close enough to hear his voice. He was talking to Cain's stone, asking him if I knew his secret." I pause, trying my best to keep myself together. I pull the folded up letter from my pocket—I've been carrying it with me since I found it, and I shake it at her. "This secret. It's his betrayal of me—an affair. I'm sure of it." Turning back to the closet, I stuff the letter back in my pocket and put my hands on my hips. I look at his now-empty shelves. "He has to have kept more than just that unfinished letter." After a few moments, I decide to search his home office. I purposely stomp on the things I've thrown on the floor. Cain stepped on my heart, so why shouldn't I step on his shoes and clothes?

Making my way to Cain's office, I swing the door open, Pace is following my every step. I realize that I have no idea where my children are, so I ask Pace.

"They're in the kitchen drawing and painting pictures."

"Thank you." I head to his desk.

"Paige, he wouldn't have had an affair. He loved you and the children. I just don't believe it."

"Well, believe it. I just can't make sense of this. I thought we had it all. Our children, careers, and I thought we respected one another!" I throw my hands in the air. "My stupidity is why I'm blindsided by this. All those nights working for the football, track, and basketball teams, was he truly working or was he off sleeping with someone?" I huff.

One by one, I pull each drawer out of his desk, dump the contents onto the desktop, toss the drawer onto the floor and sort through the pile. There's nothing but bills and unimportant crap. When I dump out the last drawer, I notice something different.

The expression on my face must change, because Pace

runs over, looks at the empty drawer, and turns to look at me like I grew another head.

"Paige, it's an empty drawer. Sit down. You don't look well."

She tries to direct me to the chair behind me, but I don't bother sitting. It's almost like I'm in a trance.

But she doesn't see what I see. One might not notice it unless they'd been pulling out each drawer and emptying the papers, pens, and... stuff. This drawer is different. It should be the same depth as the others but it's not. It's not as deep as the other drawers.

I press down on the bottom of the drawer from the inside. It gives.

"What the hell," Pace says quietly.

I glimpse up at her.

"Why would he have this secret spot?" I raise an eyebrow.

I work at the edges of the small piece of plywood until it pops out. Envelopes lay neatly compressed into two stacks. I take a deep breath, steeling myself for what I'm about to uncover.

"Are you ready for this?" Pace's question is laced with concern.

I nod, even though I'm not really ready. But I'm curious and determined to uncover any secret. Slowly, with an unsteady hand, I reach down to grab the top envelope in the stack closest to me. As I open it up, I feel Pace's breath against my neck.

Clearing my throat, I ask, "Can you give me some room?"

She slides her hand down my shoulder to give me reassurance before taking a step back. Rounding the corner of the desk, she sits down in the chair across from the desk.

Breathing one more gulp of air, I remove the papers from the envelope. It's a Mastercard bill showing several purchases of sporting equipment, shoes, and some brand name sports clothing.

Why would he hide this?

Cain has always been known to be generous, especially to his athletes. This is likely for a random student whose parents are more unfortunate than others or maybe he replaced or added some new equipment for one of the sports programs.

"I'm waiting... what is it?" Pace looks eagerly at me.

"It's a bill from a Mastercard. We don't even have a Mastercard."

"Apparently, Cain had one," Pace retorts.

I gently toss the invoice across the desk for her to look at, then I grab another envelope.

"Why would he keep something as trivial..." my voice trails off when I open the next envelope.

Pace sits up, leaning over the desk, peeking at the letter in my hand.

"Holy cow!" Pace exclaims.

The door flies open as Ivory runs in.

"Mommy, Mommy." Jameson is running behind her with paint covering his little hand. "Make him stop!" She screams trying to dodge Jameson.

"Jameson, stop that!" I say with force.

Ivory is hiding behind me while Jameson is smiling, trying to touch her.

I hold out my hand to grab him but Jameson trips, landing his hand right on my boob. Pulling him upright, I'm fuming because now not only does my boob have paint on it but so does the letter I was about to read. The paint is smeared across the letter making it almost impossible to decipher.

"Jameson, go wash your hands right now," I yell out.

He starts to cry and I want to kick myself for being so

upset. Being angry at the kids is no way to behave and it's definitely not their fault for my bad mood.

"Ivory, go help your brother," I huff.

They both leave with crushed feelings from my scolding. I throw my head back then lean forward to rest my elbows on the papers strewn atop the desk. I plant my face in my hands—not especially ladylike but it feels appropriate.

"Oh god. I must be going crazy."

"You've been under so much stress. *Sigh*. It's natural to feel… angry with everything that's happened to you. Here…" She walks to my side, turns my chair to face her, and kneels in front of me. Gently, she pulls the letter out of my hand. "Let this be. Is it really worth stressing yourself out? You have the children to think about. He's gone, Paige. There's nothing you could do now even if you find out he was having an affair."

Tears pool in my eyes.

"Oh Pace," I press the tips of my fingers into my eyes. "I'm a mess. I've not been able to sleep in weeks. Not since I found that stupid letter."

Pace wraps her arms around me and I let the tears fall.

I've only allowed myself to cry a handful of times since the beginning of our nightmare. I had to be strong. I needed to be strong for him, for the kids, and for myself… but now… I want to allow myself to be vulnerable for a brief moment. Then, I want to wash away the old and begin anew.

"Get it out. It's not going to do you any good keeping your emotions bundled up inside."

So, I do. I cry till my head aches. I cry till I have no more tears, till I'm dehydrated and start to hiccup.

When I'm done, I wipe my tears and my nose with my sleeve and decide that, for now, it's best to stop trying to find out Cain's secret or if he even had one.

"Do you feel better?" Pace asks.

A small smile appears on my lips. My sister and I have had the best relationship since my mom brought her into this big world. I can't believe I spent five years without her.

"Yeah, I do," I reply softly. "What time is it?"

Pace glances at her watch, "It's almost six."

"I was supposed to have dinner tonight with my group, but I don't have to go."

"No, you're not canceling. You need to go. I've got the kids. Who, by the way, are way too quiet." She lifts an eyebrow. "Do you think we should dispatch the military?"

We laugh.

"Knowing those two... yes. We might need all the armed forces to go in for a sneak attack."

CHAPTER ELEVEN

Paige

I sip on my water while I listen to the conversations going on around me. There's chatter about grandkids and some are talking about how their plants need to be repotted. Johnny, who's around my age, talks about going back to college. His wife died over a year ago. It's been eight months now since Cain passed. I've done my best to put the past in the past. I've done what my sister suggested and try not to worry about whether Cain had an affair. But I can't say it doesn't pass through my mind at least once a day. It's torture... the unknowing.

"Paige, you've been awfully quiet," Johnny comments.

I give him a half smile.

"I'm just listening."

Johnny tilts his body toward me, "I'm a great listener if you ever want to talk."

The last few times our group has met, Johnny has always found a seat beside me. Dating within the group is not recommended but that doesn't mean it doesn't happen. I don't even think I'm ready to date. I'm still in my mourning stage or maybe it's the confused stage. Either way, I'm not really interested in Johnny other than a friend.

Buzz, buzz.

Sitting up to dig my phone out of my small crossbody, I silently thank God for the interruption.

"Oh umm, I have to get this." I'm not lying, it's my mother-in-law. Cain's mother never calls unless something is wrong, so naturally my mind jumps to the worst thought —something is wrong at home.

I get up and make my way to the hallway that leads to the restrooms.

"Hey. Please tell me this is a friendly call," the words stream out before I can stop them.

"Oh honey, this is more than a friendly call. Callie is having her baby!" She says, her excitement ringing through the line. "Bring the kids! I know they'll want to meet their new baby cousin. She's in Saint Bernards, room three forty. We're all waiting here, so excited over the baby getting here," she squeals.

I hang up the phone and rest against the wall.

We're all waiting here... Who is all there? No, Cade won't be there, I'm sure of it.

Pushing off the wall, I stride back to the table to retrieve my purse. Johnny is watching me as I approach.

"Important call? I hope everything is well."

"My sister-in-law is having her baby, so I'm leaving." I grab my purse.

"Are you leaving?" Katie asks.

She came in late and had to take a seat at the end of the table far from me. I tried to save the seat next to me, but Johnny grabbed it when Opal had me in a deep conversation about her flower bed. My attention was solely on how her flowers were cross-pollinating. Who knew that was even a thing.

"Callie is having her baby. I need to grab my kids so they

can meet the new bundle of joy."

I smile when I think about how excited Ivory and Jameson are going to be to finally be big cousins. More Ivory than Jameson, but he'll still be excited.

"So exciting. Let me know if it's a boy or girl."

"I will."

Callie and Jack were waiting till the birth to find out the sex of the baby. I'm still shocked that Jack agreed to wait. During the whole time they were trying to get pregnant, all he talked about was having a girl. He couldn't wait to see a younger version of Callie tugging on his pants leg.

The hospital lobby's door slides open and the kids and I head for the elevator to go to the maternity floor. When the doors open on the fourth floor, Ivory and Jameson shoot out and run into the arms of Cain's parents.

"There's my grandbabies!" Cain's dad says joyfully.

"Pawpaw," Jameson pulls at his shirt pocket. Cain's dad always has candy in his pocket, and Jameson's chubby fingers find a small pack of gum.

"Really, Pawpaw?" I laugh. "Could you put some fruit in your pocket instead of candy?" I joke.

He looks at Jameson, "What fun would that be? Right, buddy?"

I giggle, knowing that saying anything is pointless.

"Has she had him yet?"

"Nope. She hasn't had *her*, yet." Jack's parents say.

I see it's not just Jack that wants a girl.

A deep voice sings from behind me.

"Here, Mom, your coffee."

Memories that I drowned years ago suddenly resurface at

hearing that deep voice. Memories of Cade being a free spirit when we were growing up. Never caring what others thought of him. How his gray eyes had shone like diamonds, especially when he was up to no good—like the time we rolled houses when we were in high school. Cade and I had paired off to wrap Kellie's house, and we'd left shaving cream-covered clumps of toilet paper covering her front porch.

I turn to stare at him. He and Cain had looked identical when they were younger, but now Cade's jaw line is as sharp as his wit had always been. And his shoulders seem wider and his legs longer than I remember.

"Hello Paige," that deep rumble says to me. His voice has always grabbed a hold of my insides and twisted them up into knots.

"Cade." I state his name as if I hadn't seen him in the graveyard several weeks ago. As if his mere presence doesn't unnerve me.

Ivory runs over, taking a hold of Cade's leg. I reach for her to pull her away from him, only Cade beats me. He picks her up, his eyes lit up with joy.

My suspicions about Cade sneaking around to see my children are confirmed. They look too cozy to have met for the first time.

Ms. Lambert did tell me a while ago that a man had been coming during Ivory's end-of-day recess, but she had no idea who he was. I would bet on Cain's grave that it was Cade.

"Ivory," I reach for her, wanting her to get away from Cade. But instead of letting me pull her away, she hunches into his shoulder. I purse my lips together, angry that a small part of me loves to see her uncle holding her. The sad part is that I can't let that happen. I know Cade is into things that even the devil would shy away from. "Ivory

Staton," I say firmly as I grab her, this time tightening my grip. "Get down. You do not go up to strangers. You don't even know him." I play the stupid card.

"But I do, Mommy."

I pretend to be shocked.

"He comes to my school and we played at the museum together when Aunt Pace took us."

There it is. The truth.

With my hands still on Ivory, I take her into my arms and walk away so I can have a conversation in private with my daughter.

I take the chair that's as far away as possible from everyone, setting her down in my lap.

"Remember when I've told you about stranger danger?"

She nods.

"How did you know Cade wasn't danger? You know what I meant when I said not everyone wants to be a good friend."

She nods.

"Then tell me."

"His eyes Mommy. They're just like Daddy's. They're kind."

I wish I could tell her differently, but I don't want to break her heart.

"Okay, okay." I inhale. "When you're at school you need to play with your friends. Not standing off to the side talking to him. Understood?" I give her a warning with a stern look.

She nods, swallowing.

"And no more talking to strangers just because they have kind eyes. Ted Bundy had nice eyes but it didn't make him friendly."

"Who?"

"Nothing. Forget I said that last part. Just don't try to be friends with someone that's not your age. Only weirdos want to be friends with small little girls. Got it?"

"Yes," she answers, but looks confused at my words.

Weirdos is not a word that I've ever said to her, but right now it's the only one that I can think of to put a little fear in her. But I can tell from the way she's looking at me that she just doesn't understand what I'm trying to say. I'll go with it for now. I'm just trying to protect her because Cade... he won't stick around. Then I'll be trying to help my daughter and my son heal another broken heart caused by a man leaving them.

"The baby's here!" Jack comes toward us with a huge, infectious smile.

I'm guessing it was a girl

CHAPTER TWELVE
Paige

It's the end of the work week and I can't believe how it's flown by. After the last student leaves my room, I stand out beside my classroom door watching children rush away, eager for the weekend. Some of them I'm sure I'll be seeing tomorrow, which happens to be the dreaded Saturday.

Our annual festival to raise money begins early in the morning. The school has been hosting the event for five years now and every year the event gets larger. Which is a great thing—unless you're working it. It's gruesome and tiring.

I waited till the last day to sign up to volunteer, hopeful that all the jobs would be taken. Unfortunately for me, there was only one position left, and I couldn't walk away when the principal came up at the very moment I was looking at the sign up sheet. He patiently watched me fill in my name for the dreaded bingo table.

Ugh, why did I have to feel so guilty that I signed up?

"See you tomorrow, Mrs. Staton," Kyle says as he runs down the hall.

"No running," I shout. It doesn't matter if I shout at him

or twist his ear, that kid doesn't listen to anyone.

Maybe tomorrow I will get a chance to speak to his parents about his behavior in class. Kyle loves to pick on the little girl that sits in front of him. He keeps pulling Daisy's hair and plays keep away with her homework. I swear, that kid has got to have the biggest crush on her. But it's evident that Daisy doesn't return the same feelings, and that's why I need to speak to his parents so they can point him in the right direction.

I hurry back into my classroom to put everything away. After gathering the test papers from each desk and stuffing them into my briefcase, I sling my purse over my shoulder and hurry out the door.

The traffic today between the middle and primary schools is a nightmare. The lady in the car behind me starts honking, pointing her finger at me... jeez, impatient people really are the worst. Clearly, she can see I'm also stuck in the same line as her, waiting our turn. The traffic makes what should have been a five-minute drive into a twenty-minute drive.

When I finally park in the teachers' parking lot at the primary school, I rush in to find Ms. Lambert waiting for me again, just as I expected.

Here come the questions.

Who is that man? Do I need to call the police? Is it safe for Ivory to be talking to strangers?

I've done my best to avoid her questions these past few days. Then there's the matter of Ivory who, despite my conversation with her to use play time to be with friends and not with Cade, still chooses to spend it with him. I've been hesitant about talking to Cade but I don't have a choice now. At the hospital, I'd made sure we were never put in a situation where we'd be alone. He's too much of a risk to be around my children. He hurts everyone that gets close to him. I won't let that happen to Ivory and Jameson.

"Paige, can I talk to you in private?" Ms. Lambert's eyes swipe between me and Ivory.

I exhale, knowing it's going to be the same conversation we've had several times already.

"Ms. Lambert, there's nothing to fear. Mr. Staton is Ivory's uncle. However, if he's interrupting play time for all the students, I'll be happy to tell him that he needs to stop coming by."

She blinks. "He's, her uncle?"

This is the first time I've told Ms. Lambert of the relationship but can she not see the resemblance? Surely she must remember what Cain looked like—we all worked together for years. Yes, Cain had had a slender build where Cade is built with wide shoulders and long legs that could wrap around a hundred-year-old oak tree. But the resemblance between the two is still unmissable.

"This has nothing to do with him personally." Ms. Lambert startles me out of my daydream. "It has more to do with him coaching her how to fight."

"To what? Fight?" My eyes cross over to Ivory, who's cowering at her desk.

"Yes, Ivory got into a fight with a boy during play time today."

"Fighting with words?"

Ms. Lambert shakes her head, "No. She used her fist. Honestly," she lowers her voice to a whisper low enough that Ivory can't hear. "The little boy is bit of a turd and deserves what he got. I'm not supposed to say that, obviously, but I still have to write her up. I hope you understand."

"I do." Being a teacher, I know you have to be fair to both sides.

Something she said suddenly piques my interest.

"What makes you say Mr. Staton has been coaching her?"

"He was standing at the fence yelling to her about how to throw her fist."

I can feel my eyes widen and my face flush. A burning sensation rises up from my neck.

Fighting is not the way Cain and I had taught her to behave. Cade teaching my daughter to fight and pick on other children is completely unacceptable. He and I will be having words.

"Ivory, let's go get your brother," I say firmly.

She slowly peels herself out of the chair and walks to me.

"We'll talk about this when we get home," I tell her. "Ms. Lambert, thank you. I'll take care of it."

"I hope you..."

I don't bother listening any further. I grab Ivory's hand, almost yanking it out of her socket. Then off we go to gather her brother.

As I load the kids up, my thoughts scatter in a million directions. How could Cade think it's okay for him to come back into my life, our lives, after all this time? How can he justify teaching a young child to fight? He's been gone for years and never once did he bother to come to a birthday party, send a card, or even call to speak to anyone.

When I pull out of the school's parking lot, I notice a black sports car with black-out windows parked along the street. It's the same car that I saw in the parking lot at the cemetery. I'm certain of it.

Cade.

I check my rear view mirror; there's no one behind me or headed toward me. Slowing my car down, I cross into the other lane and pull up alongside his car until our driver side windows are only eighteen inches apart. I lower my window and wait.

You're in there, you, you... ugh, roll that window down.

I stare at my reflection in his window for what seems like several minutes until he finally lowers his window.

The smile on his stupidly gorgeous face makes my insides light up. Heavens, why does he have to be so ridiculously good looking?

He's dangerous Paige. Dangerous. His secrets hurt innocent people.

"Good afternoon, Paige." He says my name like he's savoring a bite of his favorite red velvet cake.

My god. I imagine his little black book is filled with numbers.

"Cade." I click my tongue. "Do you sit out here and stalk people all day? No, wait, you take time out to teach my soon-to-be-five-year-old daughter how to FIGHT!"

He laughs.

"This is not a joke, Cade."

"Mommy." Jameson is yelling from the back seat.

"Mommy is talking," I grit out while staring at Cade. "Do not come back to the school again. If you do, the teacher is calling the police."

Cade doesn't reply. He's eerily quiet. His jaw is set and his eyes are stormy. Not wanting to sit through this uncomfortable silence any longer I do my best to be the better person here.

"Look," I exhale.

"Mommy," Jameson is still carrying on from the back seat.

"Jameson!" I snap. Turning around in my seat, I scream.

Jameson has gotten out of his car seat, stuck his head out of his passenger side window and then somehow raised his window until it is cutting into his neck.

Unbuckling my seatbelt, I launch myself between the front seats, into the backseat. To my relief, Cade appears at Jameson's door.

"Hold onto him, I'm going to slowly open the door," Cade says with worry in his voice.

My hands slide under Jameson's armpits. When Cade opens the door, I follow with my hands still firmly holding Jameson. Once I'm standing outside the car, holding Jameson up securely, Cade slowly rolls down the window, allowing Jameson to drop back into my arms.

My breathing is erratic, and I hold on so tight to Jameson that he is crying from my fingers digging into him.

Tears roll off my face as I hug my baby tight. The thought of losing him feels like a dagger has punctured one of my lungs, and I'm having trouble breathing.

"He's okay," Cade's deep voice says.

A small nod is the only form of communication I give Cade. I press my face into Jameson neck. Thank goodness he's safe. *Did I fasten his seat up properly?* If I hadn't been so upset over Cade teaching Ivory to fight, Jameson wouldn't have been able to crawl out of his seat.

"Okay," I sniffle.

I hadn't realized Cade had wrapped himself around Jameson and I until his lips brush against the shell of my ear. His breath dances across my skin, making my body react in ways it shouldn't.

He's not the person you knew long ago.

Clearing my throat, I catch his attention enough for him to drop his arms. For some unexplainable reason, I'm disappointed when he looks away. I want to look into his eyes, to see if there is any hint of the boy I knew so long ago. Then again, no matter how much I stare into his eyes, it won't change the past.

I say into Jameson's ear, "Let's get you back into your seat. This time I'm making sure we buckle you in nice and tight."

Cade offers to help but I don't accept it. To keep Cade at arm's length—physically and emotionally, would be best for all of us. He needs to deal with what some men would consider baggage.

Thank goodness Cain was never that way.

"Cade, I'm having a party for my birthday!" Ivory bursts out in an oh-so-happy tone. She is obviously over any panic she may have felt at Jameson's predicament.

No, no, no.

"Are you buckled up?" I say, trying to interrupt Ivory and prevent her from inviting Cade. I just know she's about to invite him and I can't afford to have him in my home.

"Birthday, huh?" Cade says trying to get more information out of Ivory.

"I really must be going. Thank you for your help." After I double check Jameson's seat belt, I shut his door and hurry to the driver's side.

Before I open my door, I stop, take a breath, and turn to Cade. "Please refrain from interrupting Ivory during play time at school. Her teacher really is going to call the police if you don't. You can understand, can't you? She's just trying to protect all the children and teach them about stranger danger."

He gives me a slow nod.

I get a feeling Cade Staton is not easy to control, even when kind words are used.

CHAPTER THIRTEEN

Paige

My eyes open to half mast when my alarm blares. Extending my arm, I feel for my cell phone to turn off the annoying sound before it wakes Pace. Groaning at the slight chill in the room, I jerk my arm back under the covers.

Ugh, I do not want to get out from my warm bed.

Pace spent the night since I have to get up so early for the festival today. She's going to bring the children after breakfast so they can enjoy the games, and arts and crafts. It felt a little odd having another person in the bed with me last night, but there is no guest room in our house.

"Why, oh why?" She complains. It appears I didn't shut the alarm off quickly enough. Lying next to me she throws the cover over her head and scoots down further in the bed.

"There's not even any light in the room," I say, with amusement in my voice. "These black-out curtains were well worth the money." I look over at her, all balled up under the covers.

"Don't talk to me. Not yet. I need more sleep and coffee before I can have a conversation with anyone."

I laugh.

Pace has never been a morning person. When she was little, Mother would have to wait till we were ready to run out the door before she would dress her. If she didn't, Pace would always find her way back into her bed. Thank goodness my children didn't inherit that trait from their aunt.

Sliding out of the bed, I grab a shower, a small healthy breakfast, and yell to Pace before I head out the door, "Don't forget to be there by lunch time so the kids can participate in the sack race."

I hear grumbles from under the covers, and shut the door so she can have a few more minutes to herself. The kids will be waking up soon. Breakfast will be the first thing on their little minds before they turn the television on to watch cartoons.

Ten minutes is all I have to myself in the car for a pep talk. I'm trying to manifest today to be a good one instead of dreading the notorious bingo table.

When I arrive, I wrap all the prizes, thinking it will make it more fun for the contestants to unwrap a prize instead of being disappointed if they were to see a food strainer coming their way.

The first thirty minutes of bingo are brutal. Every grandpa, memaw, and gigi in town has come out today to give it their best to win a golden prize. When I say golden prize, I mean crap that only your grandparents would use. Whoever set up this table knew exactly who would be running over to play.

Everything was going well, until the first fight broke out. Over a seat warmer!

When GiGi, who I thought was a sweet old lady, yelled *Bingo* and unwrapped her prize, Memaw in the back row threw her potato chips at her, exclaiming she needed it more because of her hemorrhoids. Then she went into great detail about how flared up they were. I prayed for temporary deafness because no one needed to hear how they protrude out of her butt.

GiGi laughed in her face and cheerfully told Memaw that it serves her right because she was a pain in the ass to everyone around her. Needless to say, it got really ugly from there. Words started flying in the air like bullets in a shoot out. I never heard such foul language coming from grandmothers.

Security came rushing over and locked GiGi down, but Memaw refused to budge. One of the young men, who looked like he was a high school senior, tried to pry her wrinkled fingers off the desk. When he gave up, they went with another plan of action. They picked up the desk and chair, with Memaw screaming and cussing, and carried her off.

Wow—she had quite the grip on that desk. Too bad it's not reality she has a grip on!

I give a silent, *Thank fuck!* I thought the contents of my stomach were going to come back up. My nerves were standing on edge during the showdown. I've never had a front row seat to an all-out brawl. Now I have an idea of what it was like back in the wild west, except this one was granny style.

Gossip breaks out and everyone is talking. I can hear the thick whispers from the cake walk, which is filled with participants. The sound of loud laughter vibrates though the air as they rehash the granny showdown. Apparently, there's been a family feud between them for years.

After the excitement dies down, we begin our fourth round of bingo. I'm checking my watch, praying for lunch time to hurry up.

Handing out a few cards to some new contestants, I freeze when I step up in front of Cade. He must have slipped in when I wasn't paying attention, too caught up listening to the crowd chatter about the feud between GiGi and Memaw.

"You play bingo?" It's not the most clever sarcastic remark, but I can't stop myself.

I raise an eyebrow, waiting on him to speak.

Cade looks at me, his eyes not betraying any emotion. They are cold, dispassionate, but what's scariest is how controlled and emotionless they are. The Cade I knew had a caring, outgoing, and loving character. This man in front of me isn't the Cade I grew up with.

"Are you going to talk?"

He stares at me, extends his arm with his palm face up.

It doesn't dawn on me what he's waiting for. I'm too busy noticing how he looks like someone poured him into the desk. Seriously, he's way too big for it.

My elderly contestants notice the face off between us, and GiGi's friend, who is still playing a desk full of bingo cards, yells out, "Are you going to give him a bingo card or jump his bones, because we're not getting any younger over here."

The group of elders laughs at my expense.

Great.

GiGi's friend continues with a loud comment to the lady on her left, "I'd jump his bones."

I shake my head and grimace. Older women are so much bolder. I guess when you get to a certain age you've had enough B.S. and your give-a-damn breaks.

"Here," I shove the card in my hand at him.

Embarrassed, I scurry away but not before I hear Cade chuckle.

I begin the game, calling out each ball's letter and number. Before I even realize it there is only one prize left and we're on our last game.

"I9," I call out.

A deep baritone voice bellows out from the back row, "Bingo."

It's the same baritone that has made the hairs on my neck and arms rise every time I've heard it these last few days. I keep telling myself it has nothing to do with attraction. It's the fact that he and Cain were identical twins and my affection toward my husband is somehow affecting how my body is reacting to Cade.

I pick up he last prize and set it on Cade's desk, then I turn and walk back to the podium saying, "Thank you all for coming out today. The staff is grateful for all the support you offer." I look at everyone's face, trying to make sure they all can see a genuine heartfelt thank you in my tone and eyes. "Don't forget to sign up for the door prizes if you haven't already. They're located by the Fried Oreo food truck." I point to the location of the truck. "Again, thank you all. Enjoy the festivities!" I say the last three words with way more spunk than I should.

A man calls out my name, "Paige."

It's not the baritone that sends tingles down my spine. It's more of a higher pitched voice. There's no mistaking it — it's Johnny from the support group.

"Hey," he says as he gives me a once over that makes me want to take a shower. "I didn't know you were going to be here." He spots the bingo cards in my hands. "Are you playing?"

"Hmm… no. Actually we just finished. I'm about to head over to the sack race."

A large presence closes in behind me and his shadow swallows mine. Cade's featherlight touch comes to rest on my lower back before his deep voice carries to my ears.

"Ready to go?"

It's not a question, though, it's more of a statement. It's the way he says it, like he's trying to prove to Johnny that I'm not for the taking. I'm owned by the memories of Cain—although I'm not sure that's how Cade sees it.

I clear my throat. There's already been one showdown and I don't need to have a front row seat to another.

"Johnny," I lift my hand to introduce them to each other. "This is Cade Staton, my brother-in-law." I look over my shoulder at the man whose large frame seems poised to pounce. "Johnny is in my support group. His wife past last year."

"Sorry for your loss. You must miss her dearly." Cade's voice sends a silent threat.

Johnny must get the message because he starts to fidget. The silence is suffocating and when a red-haired boy runs up to Johnny, I welcome the disruption.

"Mrs. Staton," Kyle exclaims as he hugs Johnny's waist.

I blink at the surprise.

"You're Kyle's father?" I know I have a dumbfounded look on my face but I would have never assumed Kyle was his son. I've never heard him mention having any children.

"Yep," he smiles down at Kyle. "My one and only."

I had wanted to speak to Kyle's parents about his behavior but I can't bring myself to do it now. Especially knowing about his mother's death—how she committed suicide after asking for a divorce. I'm still uneasy about the story Johnny told during a meeting. It just doesn't seem to add up. If she was looking forward to being single, why take your life?

"Well, if you'll excuse me. I really must be going. I see my sister." I'm not proud of myself for leaving Johnny there and I'm not happy with Cade for trying to redirect me away from Johnny. However, I am relieved Cade was there to help turn Johnny away. If today had marked the fifth anniversary of Cain's death, I still wouldn't be interested in Johnny.

I almost jog over to my babies, I'm walking so fast. "Hey pumpkins!" I squeal. Seeing them after the morning I've had makes my insides light up. "Ivory, are you ready for the sack race?"

She bobs her head up and down. "YES!" she says with high spirits.

"That's my girl!" I exclaim.

"I need a partner."

Cade's voice sends my heart racing. My hand flies to my chest to stop the pounding. He doesn't notice my reaction, though—he's too busy laughing with Ivory.Or are they laughing at my reaction?

"Mommy almost pee-peed at the sound of my voice," Cade tells Ivory.

They are definitely laughing at me.

Mommy? Really?

I watch them in amazement. How did those two become such friends? It still doesn't help lessen the risk of Cade walking out of Ivory's life, but a small piece of my heart heals knowing a little piece of Cain through Cade is watching over Ivory.

Their laughter doesn't stop till Cade and Ivory have lined up for the sack race. Cade has one arm wrapped around Ivory and the other holding the burlap. He looks like an advertisement for fertility clinics. Large forearms covered with tattoos that move along his bulging blood vessels. The man must drink a ton of water to have vessels like that.

The pop of a gun goes off, and each team rushes from the starting line. It's a mad dash of jumping sacks all the way to the finish line. Every person standing on the sidelines yells out for their favorite team to go faster, push harder, to make it to the white chalk line first.

"Sissy go." Jameson yells from his perch on my hip.

Screaming along with him, Pace and I both yell out for

our team to win.

They are trailing, but Cade picks up the pace. The exertion shows in the beads of sweat dripping off his nose.

"That man," a woman in her thirties points to Cade while speaking to the lady beside her, "is overcooking my ovaries." They both eye him like he's the new flavor of the month.

I don't know why, but I feel a little annoyed at her for saying such a thing.

I'm not jealous… am I? No, no I'm not.

"You need to wipe that look of horror off your face," Pace whispers.

Scrunching up my nose, I shake my head.

"What? You thought those feelings went away when he did?" she asks.

"I don't know what you're talking about."

The crowd cheers, drawing our attention to the finish line where Johnny and Kyle cheer in excitement over winning.

Good for them.

Breathing heavily, Cade's chest rises with each deep inhale. It doesn't hurt that his t-shirt is sticking to his chest from all the droplets of sweat. The man has every woman, married or single, ogling him while he strides over. With each step, his pecs shift, drawing everyone's attention.

Ivory runs over to me. Grabbing my leg, she beams up at me.

"That was fun!" She turns her head to Cade. "Let's do it again!" she says to him, her voice filled with so much excitement.

"I think Cade needs to rest." I raise my eyebrow at him, silently asking if he needs a break. "He looks like he took a bath in his clothes." We both laugh.

"How about we walk around and check out all the other activities then we might come back… deal?" Cade suggests.

Ivory looks up at him while batting her lashes. "If you'll get me a snow cone."

When did my child get so conniving?

"Deal." Cade picks her up, giving her a kiss on the cheek.

Pace and I share a glance. We're both shocked to the core with the tenderness that Cade shows Ivory.

When he places her back down, he reaches out for Jameson. "Can I?"

My heart stops at his question.

Maybe he's ready for kids. Maybe he's ready to own up to his own child. Kip has never had a real father figure other than Cain, but he was just a stand in for Cade. Kip needs someone in his daily life.

"He's a momma's—"

Jameson tries to leap out of my arms, making me gasp. I fumble around like a wide receiver with Vaseline on his hands, thinking I'm going to drop him. Cade's large hands grab a hold of Jameson and pull him securely up to his chest.

Cade lifts his eyebrow. "You were saying?" he says with a cocky grin.

Smartass.

CHAPTER FOURTEEN

Paige

Soft snores come from the backseat; the kids fell asleep as soon as I started the drive over to Kellie's. After our busy day at the festival, the kids hadn't been ready to wake up this morning.

Yesterday was a fun day for everyone, especially for the kids. Cade acted more like the boy I once knew instead of the man that he's become. His smile radiated off him and was felt by all who were around him. It wasn't a smile plastered on his gorgeous face for show. It was sincere and filled with how much he enjoyed being around his brother's children. It made me think of how much I wish Cain could have been there, to find a common ground. Maybe then they could have buried whatever happened between them so many years ago. Now they'll never get the chance.

Kellie's house sits on the other side of town. It's small but has a large backyard. It's perfect for her and Kip.

She invited the kids to come and play with Kip for the day. I'm happily tagging along so that Kellie and I can have catch up time. It's been months since I've been to her house. Come to think about it, it's been since before Cain passed.

Lately, any visits have been when Kellie and Kip came over to our house to have dinner or just to hang out.

When I park the car, I hear a small, gravelly voice.

"We're here?" Ivory asks with sleep still in her tone.

"Yep, you ready to play?" I look in the back seat to see her nod her head. Her hair is standing up with static and I can't help but chuckle at how dang cute she is.

Once I get her out of the seat, I go to the other side of the car to retrieve her still-sleeping brother.

"Come on, brother," I whisper, raising him up out of the seat. He's built like a rock and as heavy as one. He doesn't even stir when I lay his head on my shoulder. I close the door and reach for Ivory's hand, which is clutching my shirt tail tightly.

We make our way to the front door. As we step onto the small porch, the door opens with Kellie and Kip waiting inside with grins on their faces.

"Come on in," she chirps. Her voice is high with excitement.

"Thank you," I say stepping into her house. "I'm going to lay him down on your bed. He's still so tired from yesterday."

"Yeah, that's fine," she says, although she seems a little apprehensive.

Not understanding why she's worried, I add, "When he wakes up, I'm sure he'll come find me right away."

She smooths her features and I'm hoping I put some of her concerns to rest. It's understandable that you don't want a kid trying to touch your things and messing everything up.

When she opens the bedroom door she walks over to the dresser and leans against it. I find her behavior a little strange. It's as if she's protecting something, but what could she possibly keep in plain sight that she'd need to hide from me? Maybe, it's in one of her drawers and she feels possessive over it. Either way, I'm in her house and I would never go through her things.

Once I lay Jameson down, I look back at Kellie, who still looks nervous.

"Kellie," she doesn't look my way. "Kellie, are you okay?" I walk over to where she's standing.

Behind her I catch a glimpse of a photo in a frame. It's her and Cain when we were kids. I smile.

"Are you trying to hide that photo?"

Her head whips around, "It's… it's not—"

I cut her off, "It's okay Kellie. I can look at his photo without getting upset." I go to pick up the photo and smile. "Wow, that perm you had was… just wow." I laugh.

The old photo is of her and Cain sitting on the back of his truck smiling at the camera. It had to have been taken at one of the bonfires we used to have in the woods. I don't remember seeing her at any of those gatherings, but there were some I missed because my parents were so strict. I didn't get to go out every weekend like Kellie did. Her parents didn't care what she did as long as she was out of their hair. It's a wonder she grew up to be as good a person as she is today.

She laughs and agrees with me, "I went through a stage, okay?" She laughs again.

Her eyes dance as she looks at the photo.

"I found this photo after he passed and I thought I would frame it."

Grief rolls off her. I know that feeling.

Plucking the photo out of her hand, I set it back down. "No tears today. Let's enjoy each other's company." I lace her arm though mine and pull her out of the room.

In the living room, Kip is playing with Ivory and there is a massive heap of blocks.

"Do you want to play with us?" Kip asks.

"No, you play. We're going to have some tea and chat for a while," Kellie tells him. He goes back to concentrating on building an enormous wall. "We can sit outside on the back deck. Go ahead and head out. I'll grab the glasses of tea."

"Okay." Stepping over some of the blocks on the floor, I almost trip but catch myself on the arm of the couch. The kids don't seem to notice.

Seriously. I could have really hurt myself.

As I prop my elbow on the couch arm, I notice a stack of photo frames turned face down. My curiosity gets the better of me. Nervously, I look over my shoulder and when I see no one is paying attention, I pick up the top one. It's a picture of Cain and Kip. Kip is covered in sweat with his football uniform on.

"That's me and Coach," Kip says over my shoulder, scaring the shit out of me. I jump and almost drop the frame.

"Kip," I snap. "Sorry, I didn't mean to snap. You just scared me."

"Sorry, Ms. Paige."

"It's okay." I put my hand on his shoulder, giving it a small squeeze.

"I miss him." He says with sadness in his eyes. "My mom misses him."

"We all do, but he's in a better place. A place where he's not suffering anymore."

He walks back over to his blocks and starts building what looks like a skyscraper. Picking up another frame from the pile, I turn it over. It's Cain, Kellie and Kip. This photo looks to be taken at a birthday party. There's a big piece of cake in front of Kip and he is grinning from ear to ear with an icing-covered mouth.

When was this taken?

"Here we go," Kellie says as she stops at the entryway.

"Sorry, I was umm... just curious. I hope you don't

mind."

Her eyes zero in on the frame I'm holding. She shakes her head, as if clearing her thoughts. Without meeting my eyes, she walks past me. "Let's go outside and enjoy the sun." She doesn't bother waiting; she's out the door before I lay the frames back down.

As I head outside, I turn back to look at Ivory. She looks up at me with those gray eyes I love so much. "You okay, pumpkin?"

She nods her head and goes back to knocking over the blocks and rebuilding again.

I smell the fresh air as soon as I step onto the porch. "It's so beautiful out here. I don't remember all the landscaping you've had done. Is it new?"

"Yeah." Her answer is short and devoid of any emotions she may be feeling.

Did I really upset her by looking at the pictures or is she hiding something?

"Did I do something wrong?" I ask as I sit down in the empty patio chair and reach for the glass of tea she's set on the iron mesh table.

She swallows. "I just..." Whatever it is, I can see she's upset about it. "I don't want... you know. Umm."

I place my hand over hers. "I know Cain played a father role in Kip's life. I'm not upset over the photos."

She lets out a breath. "Yes, he did." She says almost to herself. "I took them down because I didn't want you to get upset. I thought maybe if you saw them it would be weird."

"It's okay. It's your house and I know Cain loved Kip." Wiping my hands on my lap, I continue, "Did you know Cade's back in town?"

She takes another sip of tea and sets her glass on the table. "Yeah, I saw him participating in the sack race."

I'm taken aback that she didn't come over to speak to us.

But it could be she didn't want Cade to see Kip.

"You could have joined us, too."

Kellie knocks over her tea, and it spills though the mesh tabletop and onto her lap.

"Oh shit!" She jumps up. Her hands tremble as she wipes the small puddles of tea off her lap.

Maybe she didn't want Cade to see Kip.

Even though I decide to steer the conversation away from yesterday, the rest of the day still seems weird, almost off. There's a thickness in the air. Almost to the point I feel like I'm choking from unspoken words.

When we say our goodbyes, I load the children up and take a breath as I slide into the driver's seat. Frozen to my seat, I stare at Kellie's house.

I know something's off. I can sense it.

I watch as the curtain in the front window is pushed aside—just enough for someone to steal a sneak peek. Kellie's face flashes for a moment before she drops the curtain as if it's burned her hand.

Strange.

CHAPTER FIFTEEN

Cade

The doorbell chimes throughout the house, then footsteps approach the front door. I know precisely when she stops at the door. I can feel her body as it moves closer to mine.

Our bodies have always been in sync to one another. She can't deny the feeling when we touch, it's too great. I plan on reminding her today of how good we are together.

When she slowly opens the door, the pain I feel any time she's not near me begins to dissipate. Her eyes look at me, sweeping over me, like she's trying to decide if she wants to run and hide.

No more running. Not for me, not for you.

"Where should I put these?" I ask, as I step through the doorway and hold up the presents in my arms.

Today is Ivory's birthday party. I went overboard with gifts. I bought her the *American Girl* doll she told me she wanted, along with a few accessories to go with it. It doesn't hurt to win over the children in hopes of gaining points with their mother.

I didn't exactly get an invite from Paige, but I did receive one from Ivory. Paige can either kick me out or put up with my presence for the sake of not wanting to ruin the party. I'm counting on the latter.

"What are you doing here?" Paige's eyebrows are drawn together.

"I got invited…" I see Mom coming into the house from the backyard and decide to use her as an ally. "Hi, Mom."

"Cade, I'm so glad you made it." She beams.

I shift the pile of presents away from me as she wraps her arms around my waist and squeezes the breath out of me.

"So glad to have my babies…"

She stops talking because we all know why—Cain. His missing presence is the elephant in the room. It's suffocating, like the elephant is sitting on my chest. Some of the weight is from the brother I cherished long ago—my other half. The half that always had my back, the half that, no matter what—we stuck together. All that was pre-Paige. Before Paige, we were always in competition, but it was friendly, brotherly stuff. When Paige moved to town and Cain saw that I was smitten, everything changed. Cain took it upon himself to make me getting the girl a challenge.

Paige turns and walks into the kitchen. As I do my best to wrap an arm around my mother, my eyes keep track of Paige while she works on getting things prepared for the party.

Mom lets me go and takes the presents from my arms. "I'm going to set these on the birthday girl's table."

"It's about time you came to a family event," Callie calls as she walks into the room with baby Jacob.

"There's my new nephew." I open my arms wide.

"Are you not excited to see *me*?" Callie asks with a grin.

"Of course." I lean down and give her a kiss on the forehead, scooping baby Jacob out of her arms.

My eyes dart over to Paige as she starts taking food out from the refrigerator. Her hair is down, shining like satin. I imagine myself lying in bed with her, running the beautiful strands between my fingers. How it would feel as it brushed over my shoulder as her naked body pressed up against mine.

Watching her work in silence is my new favorite pastime. I wish I had a key to unlock her mind and read everything she's thinking. What would I find? Does she hate the fact I showed up or does she hate how my face reminds her of Cain? If she loved him, that can't be a bad thing.

A thump against my chest wakes me out of my lustful stare. I look down at my sister, who's glaring at me.

"What?"

"Stop it," she mumbles.

My eyebrows draw up, challenging her. "Stop what?"

"You know what you're doing."

A puff of air blows out of my mouth.

"Tell me. What am I doing?" I wait for her to call me out and, being my sister, she does just that.

"You're looking at Paige like she'll be in your bed before the end of the day. She's not a toy and you don't need to play with her emotions. It's been almost a year since our brother, her husband, died but she's still not ready to be with anyone. There's something going on with her." She turns to make sure we're still alone in the living room. "She's been... different lately."

The doorbell rings and Paige goes to open it. The living room is open to the kitchen, dining room, and foyer, giving me a good view of who is at the door. A man in a blue uniform stands with a clipboard in his hands. He's not being quiet when he speaks.

"Delivery for Mrs. Cain Sutton," he states.

"That's me."

"Please sign here," he hands over the clipboard. Once Paige has signed it, he takes it back and hands her a box and a bulky envelope.

"Stop listening," my sister schools me.

"Shh," I throw back at her. I'm trying to hear if he gives any clues about who the delivery is from.

I wince as another slap from my beloved sister lands on my chest. I'm blood but I'm beginning to think that doesn't matter to her.

"Will you stop doing that." I give her my death glare.

Our bickering has made me miss out on anything the man may have said.

"Shit."

"Stop cussing. You didn't need to hear what they are saying because it's none of your business," Callie says with her eyebrows drawn together.

"Take your child and go outside to your husband." I hold Jacob out for her to grab. Thankfully she gets the hint. By the time we get done exchanging Jacob, Paige has re-emerged from the hallway.

"Everything okay?" I follow her into the kitchen like a lost puppy. That's what I am. I'm just looking for her to throw me a bone so I can pounce on her.

Give me a sign, anything that tells me you want me too.

A tray of meats and cheese are shoved my way.

"Take these outside, place them by the bread." Paige's eyes don't meet mine. "Please," she says with her head down.

I balance the tray on one palm and use my forefinger with my other hand to tilt her face upward.

"Tell me what's wrong," I whisper. Her eyes are filled with tears, threatening to overflow. "I'm not going anywhere till I know you're okay."

She breathes out a heavy sigh. "It's..." There's hesitation in her voice. She's deciding if she trusts me enough to tell me.

If I was a man who respected limits, I would drop it. But I can't. I'm growing impatient with not being able to hold her like I want. To love her like she needs.

After another shaky breath, she speaks. "It's Ivory's party, and I don't want to ruin it."

"I'm here for you." I run my thumb over her chin and then slowly move it up to pull at her bottom lip.

She clears her throat. "Why did you come back?" She pulls out of my touch, leaving a chill on my fingertips. "Why didn't you come for the funeral, your own brother's funeral. Why come back now? Why after he's gone do you want to be in our lives?" She says the last sentence with bitterness.

"I did come. I was there… You didn't see me, but didn't you feel me watching you, wanting to cradle you? I wanted to rush to your side, hold you, give you my strength to lean on in your time of need. Paige—"

"Ivory is begging to open gifts," my mother yells from the patio door, dissolving the moment I'm having with Paige.

Paige sighs. "Let's just get through this day. It's Ivory's party."

I want to ask if we are going to talk about it later but I already know she's going to avoid it. So I'll do the only thing I know to do—and that's to not give her a choice.

CHAPTER SIXTEEN

Cade

I messed up. I should have come back sooner for her. I should have never left. There are too many should haves that could have changed the past. The problem is… I can't go back. I can't change what has already happened but I can alter the future by the choices I make today.

I noticed how she changed the subject from me to her. The imagination is a funny thing when my mind starts playing out what could be in the envelop she received. It had to be something unexpected. She's acting way too strangely.

The platter starts to wobble on my palm, so I brace my other hand under it as I walk out onto the patio. In the backyard, under a large tent, family and friends are gathered together. Fold-up chairs are placed around tables and some guests have already taken a seat. There's a huge inflatable slide several feet away from the tent and children squeal with cheer when they take a fast ride sliding down it.

Until now, only my immediate family knew I was back, so everyone stares at me, except for one person—Kellie. She's been shunning me completely. She doesn't answer my calls. She won't answer her front door, and when she sees me in public, she runs. Right now, she won't meet my eyes. She knows that I know.

After I set the tray down, I ease back up and wander over to stand beside Kellie. She's helping a boy who seems to have gotten burn marks from the inflatable slide.

"Hey," the kid says. "You look like Mr. Cain." Kellie's hand freezes.

A smile spreads across my lips because… Damn. He looks just like Cain and I did at his age. His eye color is practically a family trademark. It dominates the genes for eye color of every other partner.

"We're twins."

His eyes bulge. "Twins."

"Yep, twins." I chuckle. "You resemble me and Cain at your age. What are you about, mmm… ten?

I glance at Kellie. Her face is drawn up tight, eyes narrowed at me. Silently telling me to shut up.

Afraid I'm going to spill your secret?

She is afraid. Her posture is stiffer than a metal rod.

I'm eventually going to spill her secret in front of her son or in front of others. She knows me too well. It might be because she has the mindset of a criminal,

"Can I talk to your mom?"

"Are you going to ask her out on a date? Because if you are, I'm okay with it." He runs off.

I turn my attention to the woman standing beside me. The woman who was supposed to be a good friend to Paige.

"She still doesn't know, does she?" I ask.

Her face goes pale. Her mind is turning, wondering how I know who Kip's father is. Which is completely ridiculous, because if Kip looks like me and Cain, and I know *I'm* not the father—who else can it be, right?

She bends over, clutching her stomach before she plants herself in a seat to her right.

"Please, please don't say anything," she begs.

I grin. "Wouldn't want to ruin your relationship with the woman that you've been friends with for so long?" I tilt my head. "Shame. Were you thinking the same thing when you were fucking her husband behind her back?" The words roll off my tongue effortlessly. I couldn't have stopped them if I had tried.

"We stopped. We weren't sleeping together once they got married." She says it sheepishly. "There's no need for her to know now."

I shake my head at her lies, because I doubt it stopped once he was married.

"He may have been married, but both of your betrayals didn't stop. She sees it every time Kip is around. He looks too much like us," I point to myself, "when we were his age." A thought occurs to me and it makes my stomach roll over in nausea. "I imagine she thinks he's mine." I spit out the words like they're a bad taste on my tongue. "And I bet you haven't said a damn thing to let her know otherwise. Have you?"

She quickly scans the backyard. Grinding her teeth she lets out a long sigh. "She's never asked and I've never shared." Moving in close to me, she whispers, "Unless you want others to know how Mitch's father died, I would keep my mouth shut if I were you."

Oh, she's got balls.

A hard throbbing pounds the back of my head—a sure sign my blood pressure is at a boiling point. I snatch Kellie's arm, making her gasp, and her eyes go wide. "Don't threaten me, little girl." My voice is strained. I want to wrap my hand around her neck instead of her arm. "It only fires my appetite to rid the world of people like you." I stare into her eyes, now full of fear. Crinkling my nose, I sniff the air around us. When I close my eyes, I take a deep inhale then say, "That smell." Opening my eyes, I let her see the demons dancing behind my irises. "Your fear is intoxicating." I shove her away and smile, showing all my teeth. Letting her know my bite is worse than my words.

A gentle rustle sounds behind us, and I turn swiftly to find Paige behind me.

"I...I was trying to clean up the mess," she points down to paper plates and napkins that the breeze has blown onto the lawn. "Didn't mean to interrupt you." Her eyes bob between Kellie and me, as if she thinks there are feelings between us. There *are* feelings, but they're not the kind she thinks.

Cutting my eyes to Kellie to see if she's signaling for help, I find myself balling my fists. Pure hatred fills me and I realize I don't give a shit what people would think of me if I were to cut Kellie's throat. I'm angry. Angry that she and Cain have led everyone to think Kip's mine. I'm even angrier that she's stayed in Paige's life like a treacherous snake.

"You didn't." I brush off her false assumption of anything between me and Kellie. "We were just talking about old times."

How her and Cain were fucking behind your back.

I smile over at Kellie, who's face has turned green, worried sick by the knowledge that she has fueled the beast within me with her threat.

Worry, little girl, worry.

"Here," I bend down to help Paige pick up. "Let me."

Paige doesn't fight me. She allows me to help her.

Paige stands and calls out to Ivory to come open her gifts. Once Ivory has taken a seat in front of everyone, she begins eagerly opening her gifts, thanking everyone as she's instructed to do by Paige.

Paige pulls out a package from behind the table. A tear slides down her face.

"This one came today. It's from Daddy." Paige announces as she hands the package over to Ivory.

My eyebrows crease. *Did he set something up before he passed or did Paige get it and is just saying it's from him?*

Ivory's little face is confused but she tears into the package excitedly. Paper flies in the air as she rips through it. When Paige cuts the tape that secures the contents in a brown box, a giant smile blankets Ivory's face. She squeals, reaching into the box to pull out a Polaroid camera.

There's a quietness among the family and friends gathered in the backyard. People are going into their little huddles to discuss the gift. A gift from the grave.

When Paige sneaks away, I follow her, making each step as light as a feather. I see her bedroom door open and as I get closer I can hear her soft cries.

"Paige," my voice is soft. As I stand in the doorway, I can see her reflection in the mirror of the ensuite bathroom. I continue into the bathroom; she sees me in the mirror but she doesn't stir. So I wrap my arms around her and just hold her. I bury my nose into her hair and inhale the vanilla and lavender scent of her shampoo. She's been using the same shampoo since we were teenagers. It brought a calmness to my craziness back then, and still does.

"Tell me baby, what's wrong." My words are full of meaning. I love this woman and always have. I would have been the man she married all those years ago if Cain hadn't plotted against me.

Paige doesn't chastise me for using my old endearment for her. She just cranes her neck to the side to look up at me.

"Cain... he sent," she squeezes her eyes shut.

I gently turn her to face me then bring her body flush to mine and kiss the top of her head. This is the closest I've been to her since the night I sneaked into her bedroom. I want to embrace this feeling—bottle it up inside of my heart till I'm able to hold her again.

She lays her head on my chest and her heart beats along with mine, as if it remembers me. We're in perfect sync with each other.

"Go on. You can finish it," I coo.

"He sent me a letter and it's just so upsetting."

My brows furrow. "Can I read it?" Though I manage to keep my voice soft, my rage is building. He's still trying to hold on to her from the grave.

I feel her arm moving and glance down to see her hand slide into her pocket and pull out the letter. She holds it up to me and I take it.

Paige,

It's been almost a year since I've passed. I found this company called Precious Memories that was recommended to me by Joseph. They will help keep my memory alive for you and the kids.

I've set up three gifts to be delivered to you in the next year. The first is a necklace in the small box addressed to you.

When you open the locket, you'll find words that will encourage you to keep going everyday. To think of me and to remember our special moments.

There is also a birthday present for Ivory.

I love you, Paige. I don't recall a day that I haven't.

Never forget it. Wear this necklace and think of me always.

Love you,

Cain

A deep growl rips from my throat and startles Paige.

CHAPTER SEVENTEEN

Paige

It takes strength to not put all of my body weight onto Cade. I'm drowning with feelings for my brother-in-law that I shouldn't be having. Seeing Kellie talking to Cade, standing close to him, stirred up something inside of me. Jealousy. So I decided to come in and open the letter and the box that were delivered earlier for me. I was in complete shock when I read the letter Cain had arranged for gifts to be delivered after he'd passed away. I'd opened the box addressed to me to find a locket necklace. I'd re-folded the letter and stuffed it into my pocket, then grabbed the box for Ivory and hurried back to the party before I fell completely apart.

Now here I am, holding onto his brother and having feelings of desire for him.

A sharp growl tears though Cade's throat, making his body vibrate against mine. I startle and jump back from him.

He clears his throat, trying to hide his reaction to the letter I just handed him to read.

"Sorry."

I wipe my face with the back of my hands, then dry them

on a hand towel. "It's fine." I move out into the bedroom, grabbing the letter out of Cade's hand as I go. "I need to be getting back out there."

Cade comes to stand beside me. I can tell he's wanting to say something but I don't encourage him. I just can't be having feelings for this man. Cain's long-lost brother.

His large hand comes to rest on my shoulder blade.

In a small voice I ask, "Where have you been all these years? Why did you leave?" My eyes are looking down at the letter in my hand.

His breathing is loud, but he doesn't answer me. Taking my chances, I peer up to see his face is drawn tight.

"There you are," Pace says as she walks into the room and shatters the uncomfortable atmosphere. "Mom and Dad are leaving. They wanted to say bye." Her eyes search mine.

"I'm coming."

Cade and I share a look, unspoken words. He's not ready to tell me anything and I can't blame him. I just wish he would trust me.

Once everyone has left and I've convinced Ivory to let Jameson play with a few of her new toys, Pace comes into the kitchen to help me clean up. She's staying with me for a few days since our parents are staying at their house.

"What was that about in the bedroom between you and Cade?" she questions me.

"It's not what you think. He was just..." I exhale as I shut the dishwasher. My head drops low when I begin to speak. "I think... maybe I'm having feelings for Cade." I shake my head. "Which is improper because he's my brother-in-law." I toss the hand towel I just picked up onto the counter. I'm fumbling around as I try to decipher my feelings.

"Maybe it's just strong brotherly feelings. He's Cain's identical twin and that's got to confuse the crap out of you. Although I will say he's buffer than Cain was. Don't even get me started on those tattoos. It's like the man crawled out of a mob movie." Pace starts fanning herself. "And I wouldn't blame you if you did have those kinds of feelings because if looks could set anyone's panties on fire, his would most definitely do it. "Oh, wait!" Her mouth opens wide. "Were you guys about to get it on?" Her smile stretches from ear to ear.

I prop my hip against the counter and give her a stern look. "He came in when I was upset over the package I received today."

Right… let's just pretend I wasn't checking him out… Ugg, why am I jealous?

"What did you get?" Paige asks, bringing me back to the present. "I saw you take something to the bedroom, but I was busy with Mom. She was talking my ear off about some guy that cuts their grass. Oh heavens, Paige," she looks up to the ceiling. "She was trying her best to fix me up with her gardener. Anyway, what did you receive?"

I screw my face up. Mom is always trying to fix Pace up with strangers. Not just strangers, but men who have the weirdest obsessions.

"Ivory's birthday gift and a letter and a necklace. From Cain."

"Oh." Her eyes are shaped like full moons. "I didn't know he arranged anything like that."

Me either.

"It's just so weird. It felt like his letter was trying to persuade me that he loved me. His words were, he's never not loved me. Seriously Pace, I already knew he loved us but reading that letter just felt…off. Almost like there was a hidden meaning."

"Paige," Pace walks over and gives me her most serious facial expression. "Stop overthinking it. It was just his way of saying he loved you and the kids. If anything, he was guilty of being too good of a husband."

"Yeah. He was a great husband."

Maybe too great.

Maybe that's the problem. He might have been a great husband to the outside world, but only the ones he lived were learning the truth about the man behind the mask.

We spend the rest of the night playing board games with the children and fall asleep in the living room. The next morning, I wake up with my neck in knots.

My neck isn't the only thing with knots—my hair is overdue for some attention, and that's the reason I'm now standing outside of Kellie's salon.

The door chimes when I push it open. Treading into the waiting area, I spot Kellie's booth. It's one of the front styling seats. The client in her seat says something that makes Kellie's face light up with a bright smile. Today she looks more relaxed. The opposite of how she seemed at her house and at Ivory's party.

When Kellie catches sight of me her face falls slightly.

Why is she acting weird?

"Are you here to see me?" she asks.

Giving her a small smile, I nod. "If you don't have time to fit me in I can come back." My gaze falls on the woman in her chair, who suddenly has a sour expression on her face as she stares at me.

Did she swallow a lemon?

"Did you need a hair cut?"

My brows crease before I answer her. "Yes, I was thinking about a change. A color and cut?" I shrug.

She exhales. "Have a seat. I'm done here, just let me get Julie checked out and sweep."

Ten minutes later Kellie sits me in her seat.

"I'm thinking maybe some highlights." I look at my hair in the mirror. "I'm just looking for something different. Do you have any suggestions?"

"We could do some darker blond highlights. It would look good with your natural color."

"Sounds good."

"Let me go mix the color. Be right back."

I've always been in a hurry when I'm here. It seems like when you have children you barely have time for yourself. Today, though, Pace is home with the children so I relax and take a good look around Kellie's station. At the photos and little cute pictures her son has made her. In one of her pictures, I notice that she's wearing a gold necklace I've never seen Kellie wear before. Leaning forward, I reach for the picture and carefully unstick it from her mirror.

The picture is of Kellie and Kip at a hockey game. She's got on a crew neck sweatshirt and a gold choker is barely peeking out. Squinting my eyes, I study the necklace. A loud gasp assaults my ear drums. I startle and look around me. No one. Because it's *my* gasp at what I'm seeing. Wrapped around Kellie's neck is a name necklace, *Kay*.

I stand up and yank the hair cutting cape from my neck. It rips from the force of my pull. How could she?

"That was from a Bulls hockey game. You know how…" She says with pride as she comes back carrying the bowl of hair color.

She's happily talking while I'm freaking out over the fact that one of my best friends was sleeping with my husband.

"When?" I ask.

"That picture is about four years ago. I should put a new picture up, but we just had the best time at the game and I want to remember it." She sets the bowl of color down and begins gathering the foil and everything else she'll need for the highlights—oblivious to my distress.

"Who took the picture?" A thousand questions pop up in my mind. While my heart breaks into a million pieces.

She stiffens. "I don't remember." She answers too fast.

I don't believe you.

My hands ball up into fists, crinkling the picture. Kellie hears the soft noise and finally glances up. Her eyes widen. She's been caught and she knows it.

"It's not—"

"It's not what?" I move closer to her to stand face to face. "It's not what?" I say it again a little louder, drawing attention.

"It's not what it seems. This necklace," pulling her shirt down enough to expose her neck. The evidence of Cain's devotion to her. I want to jerk it off her neck and hope that I strangle her as I do it. That fucking necklace stares at me, laughing in my face at my ignorance.

"He called you Kay, didn't he? That's why you have a necklace with the name Kay and not Kellie. K. A. Y. Kellie Annabelle Young. I didn't even put it together till now."

"Please," she looks around at the faces that are watching us. "Let's go to the break room. I'll explain everything," she pleads.

I can't stand here any longer. Grabbing my purse, I run out the door. She doesn't bother to follow. Which is just as well, because are no words she could say that would give me any comfort. She was sleeping with Cain, my husband.

I sit in my car, traumatized, staring out the front window but not really seeing anything. I jump when a hard tap occurs on the passenger side window. Cade stands beside the SUV, giving me a small wave.

"Can I sit?" I hear his deep voice even through the closed window.

He doesn't wait on me to reply before he eases himself into the passenger seat. His cologne fills the air, bringing back memories of other times we've been this close.

"What are you doing here?"

"I was following you. You looked upset when you came out. I wanted to check on you," he tells me bluntly.

"Did you know?"

"Know what?" He plays dumb.

"That Kellie and Cain were sleeping together?" I yell. "Shit," I whisper a few moments later. "Is Kip his?" I ask myself out loud. "All this time I thought Kip was yours," I say louder. "But he's Cain's isn't he?" The look on Cade's face is all the confirmation I need.

My hands fly up, slapping at the steering wheel. I'm angry, so fucking angry. Calloused hands wrap around my wrists. Pulling my hands down, Cade holds on to me.

"Don't do this." His words are gentle but I feel anything but gentle.

I want revenge. I want Cain to be here so I can take it out on him. Before I know what I'm doing,s I twist my wrists out of Cade's hold and grab him. Pulling him closer I press my lips against his. He's resistant at first but then his lips move with mine and our tongues tangle. There's an electric current flowing through my body that has only happened with one person.

He pushes me away from him, and the feeling of being lit up inside is gone.

"Please get out of my car." Our eyes are locked in a duel. I've made a fool out of myself with the kiss. He would never believe me if I told him the feelings that have been playing out in my mind since he's come back. But so many secrets have been kept that I'm not sure I can forgive anyone.

Although he looks like he wants to say something, he doesn't. He opens the door and steps out, leaving me with a slew of painful emotions to deal with.

CHAPTER EIGHTEEN

Cade

I watch Paige's white SUV leave the salon's parking lot, and it's as if it ran over my heart on its way out. I want to take away the pain Cain has caused Paige but I know she has to heal on her own.

My steps crunch against the small gravel under my feet as I walk up to the salon's door. Stepping in, I look for Kellie but don't see her.

"Where's Kellie?" I ask the young receptionist.

Fearful stricken eyes take me in. Then she points to the back.

The curtain that hangs as a door doesn't block the sounds of Kellie's whimpers. Pushing it aside, I step into the small breakroom. "What did you say to her?" I want to know every word.

"Me!" she shouts. "I didn't want her to know. I'm the one who has so much to lose. Now everyone will find out. My son will find out Cain was his dad." Her hands slap over her face. "He's going to be so upset." Tears slide down her face.

"You have no one to blame but yourself. You and Cain made this mess."

"Yeah, well, he's not here. Now I'm going to have to deal with this crap. She probably won't ever talk to me again. This is such a mess. None of this would have happened if you hadn't come back."

"Don't blame your affair on me! Did you even stop fucking Cain when he married Paige?"

I highly doubt it.

"He was supposed to be mine. He took my virginity the night of Paige's eighteenth birthday party." She pauses and I gloat, because when I saw Cain leave the party with Kellie. I knew Paige would be mine that night. "He promised it was me he wanted. He was supposed to be mine."

I scoff. "Did he lead you to believe that?"

"He did," she asserts. "I left soon after the party for cosmetology school—by the time I figured out I was pregnant, he was engaged to Paige. He said he couldn't break off the engagement because your parents were already so upset about you leaving. He said he'd support me and the baby and I needed to wait until after he'd been married for a little while. Do you know what it was like being Paige's bridesmaid—watching the father of my child marry someone else?" Tears stream down her face and I almost feel sorry for her. Almost. "He was going to leave her, but then she got pregnant with Ivory. The second time he planned on leaving, his health took a turn that none of us saw coming."

"And you gladly let Paige take care of him. Instead of pushing for him to leave her." I shake my head.

"It's not like that," Kellie asserts. "He wouldn't leave her. I begged him." She runs her hands though her hair, making her look more deranged. "He wasn't even into her until—"

"I was." I finish her sentence. "Did you really think he would ever leave her?" I knew he wouldn't. He wouldn't take the chance of me getting what—who I wanted.

"I don't know what to think anymore. Everything is about to blow up. All because of Cain." She huffs.

"That's real typical of you, Kellie. Putting the blame on others. You've done that since we were kids. Own up to what you've done."

"Whatever, Cade. I have to go." She heads for the doorway but I block it.

"Stay away from Paige. She doesn't need you trying to make amends when she's just figuring out what a douche her husband was." I drill my eyes into hers, letting her know I mean business.

She gives a nod and I let her pass.

CHAPTER NINETEEN

Paige

The walking path to Cain's resting place looks blurry, the moisture in my eyes blending the headstones together. It's hard to tell which one would be Cain's if it wasn't for the tree that shadows his grave. Placing Cain by the tree was supposed to represent the life we had together. Instead it's the tree's shadows that best represent the man beneath the dirt. His hidden desire to be a cheating bastard.

He's not worthy of my tears and I wipe them from my eyes. He's also not worthy of the words etched into his stone. Now they're much more for show than the truth. *Loving husband and father* couldn't be further from the truth. Standing in front of his stone, I want to kick, scream, and pound my fist into it, but that wouldn't give me the same satisfaction as if he were here. How can you get resolution when they're dead?

The entire time he was sick, I took care of him. I quit my job to make sure he was properly taken care of. By me. Changing him, feeding him by hand, all when he hadn't even respected me enough to take care of my heart.

"You really did a number on everyone around you," I tell

his tombstone. "Here I was mourning for you, wanting you back, only to find out everything we had was a lie. No more, Cain Staton. No more tears. No more building you up higher than the Empire State Building. Nothing. I'm not going to act like you were the perfect husband. It's time to move on and when I walk away from here, I'm leaving you where you deserve to be. In the fucking ground."

I take one last long look at the headstone and promise myself that I'll raise my children to be of better character than their father.

It's been weeks since I've been to a support meeting, but after everything that's happened lately, I need a meeting now more than ever. I need someone to tell me how to process all the anger that's flowing through my body.

Cade has kept his distance. His last text was short and just to let me know he's giving me time to clear my head. I haven't spoken to Kellie even though she messages or calls every day. The last thing I want to do is speak to her. I'm afraid of the words that might come out of my mouth if I did.

Cain's treachery hasn't helped my mind or body. I'm doing the best I can to keep moving everyday but my struggle is not going unnoticed. I'm eating less, not sleeping, and as Pace candidly told me today, *I look like shit*. I have to eat to keep moving each day because with children there is no time to lay around and analyze what signs I missed, if I could I have been a better wife to prevent the cheating, or if our marriage was just fake from the beginning. There's so much to consider.

"Would you like to share something?" Julia asks.

"Umm," I pause. This is a grieving group not a group for

survivors of cheating spouses. "I know this may be out of the norm to talk about…"

"You're welcome to share anything." she says.

Here goes nothing.

They had nothing to say when I read them the letter I'd found proving his love affair, so hopefully they'll just let me vent.

"I recently found out my *beloved,*" I practically snarl the word, "deceased husband had an affair, with a close friend of mine, I might add." I keep my eyes focused on a paper hanging on a board. "Oh, and my husband has a son by his mistress that's older than the children we had together. I can't get closure because… he's dead. There's so much hate in me for all the lies he told. He led me to believe the boy was his brother's while all this time it was his. Cain and I would go to all his birthday parties. Have his mom—my friend, and him over for dinner. Oh my god, they would sit at our table and eat, carry on conversations like they weren't sleeping with each other." My hands ball into fists thinking of their inside jokes. "Several times he went alone to the boy's sporting events, saying he was just trying to be a father figure in his life." I scoff. "Now I know he wasn't trying to *act* like a father figure, he *was* the father figure." I slap my hands on my thighs. "I wish he was here. I wish I could gut him or chew him out. I hate him. I hate that he left me with all the bills, with all this pain he caused. I don't know how to come to terms with everything I feel." I blow out a breath. "I want revenge," I say a little lower.

A throat clears and I look up at our sweet counselor, who is giving me sad eyes.

"Forgiveness is a powerful thing. Remember: It's not for them—it's for you. Anger and hate will eat at your insides, make you unable to eat or sleep. Cause you to lose your mind. Make you so bitter, it'll ruin your other relationships.

When you decide to choose to forgive them, only then will real peace come to comfort you. And it looks like you have lost weight and those dark circles under your those beautiful doe eyes say you're not sleeping, am I right?"

She's right. The hate I have is eating away at me. But I'm not willing to forgive so easy.

"Come and sit down and eat," I tell the kids as they run around Cain's parents' back yard. Mrs. Staton asked if I would bring the kids over this afternoon. She's been missing them. Since Cain's death we haven't been over to their house as often as we used to.

"I made my famous cupcakes for my sweeties," Mrs. Staton coos.

The kids jump up in their seats when she sets down the decorative platter full of cupcakes.

"Not until you eat all your food first." I give them a stern look that makes their little faces fall. "Don't give me that look."

A soft touch on my back has me almost jumping out of my skin. Mrs. Staton giggles, "I didn't mean to scare you, honey."

"I guess I'm just a little jumpy."

"Have you been sleeping?" Mrs. Staton really looks hard at my face.

"Not really."

Your cheating son keeps me up at night.

"Go lay down in Cain's old room. I'll take care of the kids."

I know she wants to help out. I also know that as soon as I walk away she's going to hand a cupcake over to each of them. Even so, I reluctantly agree to go lay down.

I walk down the hallway, passing Callie's old bedroom.

We spent hours together in there when we were growing up doing our hair and lip syncing to the songs that came on the radio. When I make it to the bedroom that Cain and Cade had shared, I slowly open the door. The twin beds still sit in the same places they did when Cain last lived at home. The desk, chairs, and awards have been preserved like the room is a time capsule.

Pictures of me, Callie, Cain, and Cade from our high school years are pinned up on a press board.

Seems like so long ago.

As many times as I've been to his parent's house, I've never poked around in this bedroom. My finger drags along the oak desk. Nothing in the room has a speck of dust on it, which means his mom must come in here to clean. Everything in the room feels like home, but home doesn't feel the same. It feels foreign, out of my comfort zone. It's because of the secrets that have been kept for too long.

I sit on the edge of Cade's bed, kick off my shoes and lay on my side, looking at Cain's bed across the room. Inhaling the scent of the pillow that's tucked under my head and arm, I can smell Cade's cologne. The scent of cedarwood is comforting and lulls me to sleep.

The bed dips and I wake from my nap. I have to blink several times to remember where I am.

Hot breath fans over my ear and sends a wave of goosebumps rushing over my skin—not just on my neck and arms, but they go viral and cover me.

"Looks like I found Goldilocks in my bed." His deep voice vibrates against the skin on my neck. "Do you want to eat my porridge too, or have you already done that?"

My heart rate picks up and I know it's from his words. When his hand slides over my hip, I don't want to move. It's been so long since I've had a man touch me and praise me, that I'm starving for his attention.

"Are you going to answer me, Goldilocks?" His hand comes back to my hip and gives it a tight squeeze. "I guess the big bear will eat you then."

He flips me onto my back, throwing his leg over both of mine to pin me down.

I gasp. "Cade."

His grin is sin and his eyes are stormy as they roam over my face.

"You have to get off of me." I reach up to push him off but even my strongest push doesn't move him.

His eyes focus on my lips. "Go on a date with me." He uses a softer, more seductive tone than his teasing remarks when he says it.

CHAPTER TWENTY

Cade

Those beautiful doe eyes assess my intentions as she stares straight into my soul. I'm burning up with need for her. Her body is so close to mine, and it wouldn't take much to have her wilting under me. But I want more with Paige. I want the pleasure of forever with her. House, kids, I want it all.

"One date. It's all I want…for now," I tell her.

She swallows and it draws my attention back to her lips. "The kiss you gave me in your car was a familiar taste of homemade apple pie from our teenage years."

That comment earns me a smile from those beautiful lips.

"What if I say no?"

She's teasing me. I can tell by the pulling of the corner of her lip. She wants to smile but doesn't.

Bringing my lips closer to hers, I say, "Then I guess," I brush my lips against hers, "I'll tie you up and kidnap you." I pull her bottom lip with my teeth. It makes her chest rise and fall.

"Paige, are you up?" my mom yells from the door.

Paige panics, arms and long legs flying in every direction, and pushes at me. My balance goes unsteady over her and I fall between the wall and the twin bed that was mine when I lived at home. Since we only had a three bedroom home growing up Cain and I had to share a bedroom.

"Oh my god," Paige yelps.

The bedroom door opens and my mother asks Paige if she is feeling better.

"Much. Thank you. I'll be out in a minute, let me just get myself up."

"Okay, hun. We'll be in the backyard. The kids wanted to play on the new swing Kurt just finished."

When the door shuts, Paige peers over the edge of the bed, looking every bit the angel with her long dark hair hanging over both shoulders. I reach up and run my hand along the smooth strands. It's soft as a feather pillow and smooth like silk. I want nothing more than to wake up with my nose buried in it every morning.

"Umm, I... I need to go," she says with a slight stutter.

I'm treading a fine line when I raise up and press our lips together. The kiss is slow. There's not a need to hurry. It's a kiss that's filled with a desire to drag every single moment out. My yearning to be closer to her becomes greater with every stroke of our tongues.

I begin to rise up, but when the bedroom door opens without advance notice Paige pushes me away from her. She quickly wipes her lips before turning in my sister's direction.

"Callie," her voice is two pitches higher than normal.

Callie's narrows her eyes at us. She knows I've always had a thing for Paige but hasn't ever commented on it. She's great like that. Always quiet about my affairs but never hesitating to punch me in the balls when I make a mistake.

"Cade." She says my name hard. "Didn't know you were in here." She turns her attention to Paige and I can feel the air shift from stuffy to lighter as she speaks. "Paige, Mom and Dad have the kids entertained and I've pumped enough milk to feed Little Jacob for hours. Let's have some girl's time like we used to."

Paige jumps off the bed like someone lit her ass on fire. "I'm ready."

Callie disappears into the hall. Paige looks over her shoulder," moving her lips to say "No."

No isn't a word I accept.

The sun is going down when my mother calls my name. I turn my head toward her and my words get caught in my throat. She's escorting Dillion over to where I'm sitting.

Fuck! What's he doing here?

"Hey, man," he says as he takes the seat next to me.

"What the hell are you doing here?" I mutter, glancing around to make sure no one hears us.

He laughs and it doesn't sound natural.

"Wow, I thought I would get a warmer greeting than that." He raises an eyebrow. "Don't sweat it. I'm here on pleasure, not business," he says while he eyes Paige. "Holy shit! Is that her?" He looks at her with interest. A little too much interest for my liking.

"Yeah," I growl between my teeth.

"She's hot. No wonder you're wanting to quit and go soft."

"Dillion."

"Hmm."

"We're friends, but take your eyes off her before I push them back into your head."

He laughs because he thinks I'm screwing with him. I'm anything *but* screwing with him. I've always been protective when it comes to my family, and Paige is another level up. He knows that.

"Shit, I'm fucking with you. Loosen up, for real." He slaps me on the shoulder.

"What are you really doing here?" I look at his choice of clothing. His suit is hardly personal visit wear. He's here to ask me to do another job, I know it.

"I just wanted to check on you to see if you're still planning on leaving the business." His lips curl up in a friendly smile but it doesn't reach his eyes.

I'm good at finding people that don't want to be found but I'm better at reading people's body language. What his body is saying gives him away.

"Hey sweet lady!" Dillion's voice purrs.

Swinging my head, Paige stands to my left, where she's picking up Ivory's cup.

"Oh, hello again." Her voice sings. "Do you two know each other?"

The question is how does she know him?

"We're old colleagues." Dillion tells her. "We go way back."

"How do you two know each other?" I question them.

Paige stands there looking at Dillion and my jealousy hits a peak. I have to put my hands under the table to hide my fists. They want to explode on Dillion's face.

"We met at the supermarket this week...Tuesday, I believe. Umm," she points to Dillion.

"Dillion." He says his name, reminding her.

"Yes, sorry. I'm terrible with names. I shouldn't be, I'm a teacher. I think it's just adults that I have problems with remembering names." She gives him a warm smile. Turning her attention back to me, she continues. "Anyway, he asked for help with locating some spices he needed for a dish he was making. Mr. Dillion apparently is a great cook." She smiles and looks back at him.

I growl under my breath, which makes Dillion chuckle beside me. Paige must not hear it because she carries on until she's interrupted by Ivory.

"Mommy, what's taking you so long?" Ivory asks from her mother's side.

Spotting me, she runs over and climbs into my lap. "Come swing with me," she demands excitedly.

"Not yet, I'm talking to my friend." I throw my thumb up toward Dillion.

She pouts but Paige reaches her hand out for Ivory to grab a hold of it. "Let's swing one more time before we leave."

Ivory does a puppy dog face and it makes me laugh at how good it feels to be a part of their normal everyday lives.

"Go on. Do what your mother tells you." I put her down on her feet for her to run along.

Once they've left, Dillion keeps commenting on Paige's beauty. "I can see why you're so taken with her."

Keeping my face straight, I give him a warning. "Don't play with me, Dillion. I know you better than anyone. I know you don't cook and that was a lame excuse to introduce yourself to Paige. Stay away from her and my family. Nothing good can come out of you being around."

"Tsk tsk, you forget who you owe your new life to." Paige looks over to us and Dillion gives her a small wave. "Besides that, old friend, I'm not causing trouble. I'm just wanting to... stay in touch."

Not one word is true, I'm certain of it. Nothing comes for free from Dillion. He wants something, I would bet my life on it.

"I have to get going along but I'll be in touch." He pushes out of the chair. "Oh, I forgot to say goodbye to Paige. Tell her thank you for helping me in the supermarket and maybe... I'll see her around." His grin doesn't hide the hidden message in his words. Every cell in my body signals me to pay extra attention to Paige's whereabouts.

"Who was that man, son?" my dad asks, making me jump out of my deep thoughts.

"Just someone I know." I don't want to give my dad details. He used to be a detective in the city and he still has connections. I know that if he has any questions he'll dive in and find out the answers through friends.

While my father was on the right side of the law, I've been on the wrong side, making bad decisions that would hurt him, if he found out.

"He looks familiar," he says, watching Dillion leave though the backyard gate.

"Pawpaw," Jameson yells as he runs toward Dad.

"No, no, we're leaving, little man," Paige tells him.

She picks him up and he tries to wiggle his way out of her hold.

"Let me help walk you guys out." I reach for Jameson and he accepts the invite.

When they've said their goodbyes, I walk them to Paige's car. She's quiet, trying not to make eye contact as she sidesteps me to buckle the kids in. She closes the car door after the last child is secured.

"Thank you for your help," she says without making eye contact.

I back her up against her SUV and place my finger under her chin to lift her face up, forcing her to look at me. "Paige." Her eyes rise up to meet mine. The depth in them is so clear I can see her heart. "I'm not above begging. Please go out with me."

"I...I don't think that's a good idea, Cade." Her voice is so low it's barely a whisper. "What would the children think? What would your family think?"

"They'd be happy for us and if they're not, we don't have

to come around if you're not comfortable. But you can't deny this chemistry between us."

"I just..." She stalls.

"Listen, just think about it. Give it a day, sleep on it. Maybe I could come over after work one day this week and hang with you and the kids. Does that sound good? Because I'm not going to give up, not ever."

She nods and I step back, letting her go for now.

CHAPTER TWENTY-ONE

Paige

It's late at night when I get home from my meeting. The kids are already in bed and Pace is asleep on the couch. I decide to run myself a bath.

I get undressed and slip into the warm, inviting water, intentionally exhaling away all of the uncomfortable conversations from my meeting.

Ring, ring. My phone buzzes from the side of the tub. *Unknown Caller* flashes on the screen. I push the button to send it to voicemail and place it on silent. No one normally calls this late and if it's someone close to me, they'll send a text. The bath relaxes me to the point I start to doze off... except a loud banging noise startles me.

"What the—." Footsteps are padding along the hardwood in the direction of my bedroom.

When my bathroom door opens, Pace is standing there—frightened.

"Shit, someone's beating at the front door," she whispers.

"Did you look out and see who it is?" The banging begins again, making me jump out of the tub. Grabbing my silk robe, I don't even bother drying off before I wrap it around me.

"Have you got a gun?" Pace asks.

"I don't know how to shoot a gun," I hiss at her.

"Give it to me. I do."

I stand up straighter. "Who are you?"

"I'm someone that wants to defend herself if I need to. Now get the gun!"

The banging starts up again.

Without paying her any attention, I walk on tippy toes to peak out the front window, trying not to be noticed.

Relief floods me when I see Cade, and he's looking every bit as worried as we are. I open the door and he strides in.

"Why the hell haven't you been answering your phone?" he bellows, closing the door behind him.

"Keep your voice down and what is wrong with you? If it was the call I received a few minutes ago, you're calling from an unknown number. I don't answer unknown callers. If you won't let your name be seen, then you can't expect me to answer your call."

He gets closer to my face, "Always answer your phone. You don't know if it's an emergency."

He sounds like my mother.

"What is wrong with you?" I repeat. My eyebrows draw together. I've never seen Cade act so upset.

He runs his hand through his hair. "I've been worried sick."

"O... kay...There's nothing to worry about, I can assure you." He looks out the window, turning his head left to right. "What are you looking for? What is going on?" I try to stand beside him to see outside but he gives me a gentle push away from the window. "Why are you acting like this?"

He starts pacing the floor, looking at it. I can't tell if he wants to murder it or caress it.

My curiosity gets the better of me. "Why are you pacing the floor like a caged animal?"

When he abruptly stops, he raises his eyes to scan my body. I can feel the heat in them as they slowly roam up my bare legs, past the intimacy of my damp bathrobe, until they finally make it to my face. I can see in his eyes that we share the same intense *want* for each other. It's been constant now for a couple of weeks.

I try to swallow but my mouth is too dry. Still staring into each other's eyes, he takes a step toward me. Another step, then another till he's standing in front of me, breathing me in. His hand comes up in a slow rise. Large fingers brush my temple and slide to cup my face.

"Oh my god, don't tell me something's wrong," Pace says. We both jump away away from each other. I'd forgotten she was here and Cade probably didn't know.

We're both flustered and my heart is pounding. *Thump, thump thump.*

"Is somebody going to tell me what's going on? Why Cade was beating on the door like that?" Pace demands. My heart is still pounding so fast and so loud that Pace's voice seems muffled.

I yawn and rub the tragus of each ear to help clear up my hearing. "Yes, Cade, do tell us why you are here."

"Oh...I couldn't get Paige on the phone because she wouldn't pick it up." He widens his eyes for effect. "That's why I'm here." He says it with a fake smile.

I can see something is wrong. He's too antsy, pacing the floor, not knowing what to do with his hands. Tells I remember from our teen years. Something is going on and he's trying to hide it.

"Well, you can see everything is fine. So you can leave now." I open the door to call his bluff. He shuts it.

"I might as well stay since it's so late."

I check the hands on the clock hanging beside the fireplace. "It's only ten. I think you'll be okay to head home." I stand up straighter. He's not staying here. If the kids wake up, it'll leave me in an awkward position. I don't want to have to explain anything to them. This is *not* a good idea.

"I'm staying," he says with a stern look that tells me I won't be able to push him out even if I had a bulldozer to move him.

"Excuse us for a moment." I grab Pace's hand and storm back to my bedroom, dragging her behind me. "He's not going to leave—which means you can't either." I point my finger to the floor, making sure she understands me. Her grin tells me she is loving this. "When the kids wake up in the morning, they're going to ask me all kinds of questions. Okay, Ivory will be asking all the questions."

Pace throws her head back in a laugh. "Are you afraid of the kids or yourself giving in to that tempting hunk out there?" She raises an eyebrow.

I'm quiet for too long so she feels free to continue with her insinuations.

"You know… I can see a spark between you two."

"There's not a spark. It's more of a brother and sister… caring for each other."

She crosses her arms and pops a hip out. "Stop trying to fool me. I'm not a freaking kid. I can see it."

I run my hands through my hair and as I throw my head back. "Okay, okay… I'm… extremely attracted to him but I haven't worked things out in my head yet. Even if I had, I still won't or wouldn't have him stay overnight. Not when the kids are here. Please stay with me?" I clasp my hands into a praying position and bat my eyelids.

"Fine." She gives an exaggerated exhale. "Do you want me to sleep in Ivory's room so I can give you and Cade some private time?" She wiggles her eyebrows.

"The only reason I'm not going to murder you in your sleep tonight is because you're doing this for me. But don't push it. No, you're staying in my room with me. So there's not even a chance of anything happening."

CHAPTER TWENTY-TWO

Cade

My shirt is damp with anxiety-inducted sweat, so I peel it off. The cool air hits my chest, making steam rise from the blistering heat of my madness. I toss the shirt onto a chair in Paige's living room then toe off my shoes. Slumping back on the sofa, I close my eyes. I knew, just knew that Dillion was going to cause trouble.

I've made him a lot of money over the years and I was a fool for thinking he would let me walk away. When Dillion called earlier tonight and asked me to do another job, then reminded me that *bad things happen to beautiful people*, it confirmed my suspicion that he's willing to go to any extreme, including hurting Paige, to keep his cash flow going. It was a clear message that I needed to jump when he said jump.

But his threats to harm Paige only pushed forward my protective instincts. Instead of making me bend to his will, his word lit a fire in me and I rushed to Paige.

The house is quiet now. Paige and Pace went to bed an hour ago and I'm tempted to go to the bedroom to check on them. Thoughts of keeping Paige and the kids safe go round and round my mind. How can I keep them safe if I don't tell her? If I tell her, she'll hate me for bringing my world to her. But there's no way I'm going to let this keep me from trying to be with her. In the past, I let Cain direct my path, but not this time. I'm not going to let Dillion or anyone else keep me away from her. I'll do whatever is necessary to keep her and keep her safe.

I stiffen in alert as a soft scuffing noise comes from the hallway. I don't move, keeping my eyes slitted as I watch Paige walk on ballerina toes toward me. Her scent of vanilla and lavender drifts its way to my nose. I inhale slowly, wanting to make her scent last forever. It's like a drug and frees my mind of the burdens weighing on me. She does that to me. She's always been the calm to my storm. She stops at the end of the hallway, her eyes glued to my bare chest.

"Are you enjoying the view?"

She shivers at my seductive words, making her beautiful breasts bounce and her nipples harden against the fabric of her tank top. I want to say it again and slide my hand down her cotton shorts.

She crosses her arms and runs her hands up and down the sun-kissed skin of her biceps. "Put some clothes on," she hisses.

From the lust in her eyes, I can tell she doesn't mean it. Or maybe she does, since she throws a blanket at me.

"I have children. They don't need to see," she points her finger at me, waving it up and down, "all that."

I stand, and notice that my slouched position on the sofa has pushed my low-slung jeans even lower. I decide to use that to my advantage and rub my hands across my pecs and abs. I watch her eyes trail the motion. "Am I distracting you?" I grin.

Knowing she's been caught, she throws her hands up and walks into the kitchen. I don't bother putting my shirt back on. I follow her and prop my ass against the sink.

"You couldn't sleep?" I cross my arms.

"No, I..." She fills a glass with water from the fridge. Taking a large drink, she turns back to me. "Had a bad dream."

"Do you want to tell me about it?"

"My dream?" She asks like she's surprised I would want to hear it.

"Yes, your dream." I confirm. "Come on, try me. I want to know."

She breathes in and exhales even harder, then scratches her forehead as she struggles with telling me.

"Before," she meets my eyes. "Before Cain died, I used to have this dream where we were on our annual vacation at the beach. It would be like everything was normal. We were enjoying the day, the kids played, and then all of a sudden everyone disappeared." Her eyes go teary. "Now when I have the dream, the only difference is Cain's in the ocean, goofing around like he used to do when we were teenagers. You remember?"

I nod.

"Remember how scared your parents used to get when he pretended to be washed under by a current?" She shakes her head. "Your poor mother. Anyway, umm... he's out in the ocean and I'm thinking he's playing except the ocean pulls him further away from the shoreline." She takes another drink. "I'm left crying." Tears spill over her cheeks. "And it's like I'm frozen. I can't move, I can't cry out for help. But then I realize I'm not crying... I'm smiling. I'm happy that the ocean swallowed him up. What does that say about me? I'm a horrible person." She rubs her temples.

"No, you're not." I pull her into my chest and wrap my arms around her. "You're not. It's just a dream. It doesn't mean anything." I try to convince her, but what I really want to say it that the ocean should have swallowed him long ago.

"We shouldn't," she pushes to step back from me.

I miss her body being tucked into mine already. She fits perfectly into my arms.

"I can't afford to have the children see me standing close to you like that."

"It's not because you don't want to stand close to me?" I raise an eyebrow. "It's because you're worried how it will look to them? I can tell you they like me pretty well," I say with confidence.

"Stop playing games," she demands. "You don't get to come back and play with our lives." She lowers her voice. "I know, I... we never meant anything to you but I refuse to let my and Cain's children get hurt when you get an itch to scratch somewhere else."

"What are you talking about?" I stand up straight, confused by her words.

"Never mind, forget it." She puts her glass down in the sink.

I grab her by her wrist, stopping her from walking away. "I left for a good reason, but it's not one that my family would understand. But I didn't just walk away." She pulls free from me.

"Don't worry about it. I'm headed to bed. Help yourself to anything you want."

What I want is you.

Once Paige has slipped off to bed, I go back to the front window. Pulling the curtain back a hair, I spot a black SUV at the end of the driveway. My car is parked at the neighbor's house because I didn't want Dillion to know I was here. If he decided to make a bold move tonight by sneaking in, I wanted to surprise him.

The SUV's window rolls down and I can just make out

Dillion's face when the tip of his cigarette glows as he takes a drag. He flicks his cigarette out, rolls the window up, and waits. I release the curtain and pace while I go over my options. His presence here in town weighs on me. His greed, his hunger for money, is never ending. The man has to be sitting on millions of dollars but yet he's not satisfied with what he has. Always wanting more.

Buzz, buzz.

My phone vibrates on the coffee table. I pick it up, my grip tightening when I read Dillion's name and the his text.

You can't stay with her every night. Come back to work with me. I'll give you time to think about it.

Shit!

I walk over to the window and push the curtain wide open. I don't care if he sees me—he obviously already knows I'm here. His car is running now and when the window goes down the lights from the dash show me that he's grinning like the joker. I sneer at him and he gives a wave as he drives off.

CHAPTER TWENTY-THREE

Paige

I wake up to a bed full of warm bodies. Pace is tucked under the covers with Jameson laying across her body. Ivory is stretched out in the middle of the bed with one foot pushing into the middle of my back like a dull sword. I fold the cover back, getting out of the bed, and I bend backwards then forward to get the knots out. Even so, I'm still slightly hunched over as I open the bedroom door and wander down the hallway.

The smell of bacon hits me with full force.

Oh heavens that smells good!

"Coffee?" Cade asks.

"Yes, oh god, yes."

He hands me a cup and I gladly take it. "Slept wrong?"

"Mm, more like I had a foot in my back." He laughs. It sends electric currents through the air lighting up my insides.

"Do you want me to see if I can get it out for you?"

I gulp and I can't keep my eyes from dropping down to the bulge in his jeans. That sounded like an invitation for something other than rubbing the knot out of my back.

"No, I'm good." I try to blow him off.

"Sit down," he says firmly as he turns one of the kitchen chairs around so that the chair back is sideways to the table.

"You don't take no for an answer do you?"

"Not when it's something I want. Now, take a seat and I'll rub it out for you."

Shaking my head, I sit, fold my arms on the table and lay my head on them. "It's in the middle of my back."

His hands start massaging my shoulders. Soft at the start then he digs deeper until the tight muscles there relax.

"Lower, the middle of my back."

"Don't rush me. I've got my hands on you. I want to take my time."

He goes back to working my shoulders, inching his way down a little at a time. I moan, it feels so good.

"Don't do that." His voice is deeper than normal.

"I can't help it. I didn't even know I had knots in my shoulders until your hands found them."

His hands pull away and then I hear a chair scraping the floor. I raise my head, disappointed that his hands aren't still digging into my back.

"Why did you stop?"

"I have something I need to tell you." I tilt my head to the side, waiting for him to continue. "I... I want that date. It's been a year now since Cain died and I've been waiting patiently. Tell me there's a chance for us."

The air in my lungs lays heavy in my chest. Kissing him was a fantasy but I don't know if that fantasy is really meant to be.

"Talk to me," he pleads.

"Umm, I don't know." It's all I *can* say, because I really don't know. I don't know what troubles come with him. Being young and single is so different than being single with kids, a mortgage, eye-popping medical debt, and the shit that comes with day-to-day responsibilities.

"What is there not to know? That I want to spend my mornings and evenings with you and the kids?" His voice dips lower. "Then share my nights with you in a bed where we talk and laugh, and where I pleasure your body with sinfully delicious acts?"

Holy shit!

"I'm not waiting any longer. Tonight I'll pick you up around seven. I've already asked Callie if the kids can stay with her."

"You spoke to Callie about us?" I point my finger between us. He grins.

"My sister has always been able to read me better than anyone. I've never been able to hide anything from her. Don't worry." He places his hands on mine. "She's okay with it."

He sees the sweat on my forehead. Grabbing a nearby napkin, he gently dabs at it. "Don't sweat over it. I'm going to go. I did some thinking last night and you were right. The kids don't need to see me here, not yet, not until we're ready."

Wow. He's awful sure of himself.

He stands. "Yes, I am." He answers my unsaid comment.

"I didn't say anything."

"No? I read your mind. I'm sure of it. We're going to be together."

Teenager-me would have swooned at his confidence but that girl is long gone and one thing I've learned is that life can throw you a curve ball.

"Breakfast is cooked—toast, bacon, and pancakes. All you need to do is heat them up. I'm going to go. Be ready at seven."

He leaves without even trying to touch me. I watch him

walk to the living room and grab his shirt, shrugging into it as he walks to the door. Before he gets there, he turns his head, looks at me and winks.

A Chevy SUV darts into my lane of the highway, causing me to swerve onto the shoulder.

"You idiot," I mutter. The kids are in the backseat so I keep the road rage under my breath. Once I've pulled back into my lane, I look ahead and see the Chevy in front of me, weaving through the traffic. "Slow down, you're going to kill someone."

As if the driver heard me, the car's brake lights come on and the drive pulls onto the shoulder. I glance at the SUV as we speed past, but I can't get a good look at the driver. Even so, I repeat my earlier sentiment. "Idiot."

"What did you say, Mommy?" Ivory asks from the backseat.

"Nothing baby." *Always listening.* My gas gauge beeps, alerting me that I'm low on fuel. *Crap.* I wasn't planning on making any stops. I'm dropping the kids off at Callie's then heading back to my house to meet Cade for the date I seem to have been told I was going on.

I flick my blinker on and pull over at a station to fill up. I don't know what happened to all the mom-and-pop gas stations—where the guy would come out and ask how much, then pump your gas for you. I wish they were still around.

I unbuckle and then look back at the kids playing on their tablets. What would we do without technology to keep children entertained? Oh yeah, drive straight into a tree because they would be asking *are we there yet* every five minutes.

"I'll be back, got to get gas." *Silence.*

I grab my gas card and hop out, locking the doors in the process. I'm the definition of a mother hen. Yep, my picture is below the word, the pronoun, and the definition.

"Hey, I know you," a familiar voice says.

When I turn around, I almost bump faces with the man I met at the store and again at my in-laws'.

"Oh hey. Sorry, I didn't see you standing there." *Seriously, can you take a step back?* Very close talker, too close.

"Dillion," he points to himself. "I thought that was you." He looks in the backseat, making the hairs on my arms stand up. *Something isn't right about this guy.*

"Yep, it's me," he says, redirecting his attention to me and not my children.

"Cute kids." He says it in a way too friendly tone.

"Thank you." We stare at each other. *Umm, you need to walk off.*

He doesn't take the hint. Still standing too close, with almost nothing between us but silence, he rocks on his toes, waiting on what, I have no idea.

"So, how do you know Cade?"

He smiles.

He just got what he wanted. He wanted me to ask about him and Cade.

"Oh, we go way back." His eyes light up. "But we work together… head hunting business." He grins. I bite back the gasp wanting to escape.

This man is pure evil. Is Cade the same?

"I need to be going. Big date tonight." He walks off, taking one more look at me over his shoulder.

Finally, I'm able to relax and I start to pump my gas.

"Hey Paige, have fun tonight!"

A chill runs down my spine as I look up to see Dillion

getting into the same Chevy SUV that ran me off the road.

With a wave, he closes his door and pulls out of the station.

CHAPTER TWENTY-FOUR

Cade

My car hums to a stop in Paige's driveway. Turning off the ignition, I take a look at her house. It's a small, modest, one-level home with a brick overlay. There's a bay window in front where the dining room is. The baby blue paint on the porch pulls out the color on the brick. Baby blue was always Paige's favorite color. I wonder if Cain ever knew that.

Getting out of my car, I walk to the door and ring the bell. Tonight the air is warmer than normal but it matches how I feel for my date. I've been waiting for what feels like an eternity to be with Paige.

Heels click along the hardwood but not as fast as my heart beats as the sound comes closer to the front door. The front door opens with a swift movement and I think I've just died because I've never seen anyone looking more like an angel. Paige's dark hair is pulled to one side over her shoulder and she's wearing a dress that's more casual, but sexy as hell at the same time.

"Wow." The word escapes my lips in a strong huff, as if propelled by my rapid heart beats. "You look amazing." My eyes sweep over her, examining every centimeter of her.

"Thank you," she says shyly.

"Are you ready?" As much as I would love to walk in, pick Paige up, throw her over my shoulder and carry her to her bed to eat her, I want to show her I am her other half. The half that was kept from her for too long.

"Yes, let me grab my purse."

Once she has her purse, we load up in my car. The conversation is easy. We talk about her children and her job, and we talk about what all has changed in our small town of Haydenville.

"Where are we headed?" she asks.

"I thought we would try that new restaurant, Flames. I read the reviews in the town news and they got five stars." I say this while stealing looks at her toned legs.

"Callie was telling me about it. She and Jack went to it last week."

"Yeah, she's the one who mentioned it," I tell her.

"Does she know we're on a date?"

"I couldn't sneeze without her knowing or her trying to get up in my business." My sister is always the first one to find out about everything. It still surprises me how she had no idea that Cain had a child with Kellie.

Paige doesn't say anything when I mention Callie. I wonder if she thinks Callie knew about Kellie?

"You know, she didn't know about Kip," I say, hoping she'll tell me.

Still looking out the window, Paige brushes her hands down her skirt making my eyes trail the movement.

My god, those legs could be used in a commercial for shaving cream, pantyhose, or just about anything. Or they could be wrapped around my neck...

"I know... it's just... never mind." She brushes off what she was going to say.

"You can talk to me."

Shaking her head she says, "It doesn't matter anymore."

We pull into the parking lot and I find a space close to the front door. Shutting the engine off, I turn to Paige and place my hand on her head rest and then lean toward her.

"What matters is you. If it bothers you, then I want to be the first one you want to tell. If you want to talk." I look into her eyes and see the pain that she's trying to force back down.

"When I went to visit Cain's grave, you were there. I heard you say, *Does she know your secret?* Was that it? Was it Kip?"

"Let's go get a table and we'll talk." She puts her hand on my leg, halting me from opening my door.

"Please tell me. Did you know?"

I shake my head. "I didn't know about Kip. I knew Cain was sleeping with Kellie but I couldn't say anything. He..." I rub my hands together. They're sweaty, my fear of telling Paige everything about me is overpowering. What will she think of me when I tell her what I've done? Will she let her kids be around me? Will she want to be around me? If there's one thing I hate more than a thief, it's a liar. Little lies can lead to bigger ones and soon they're too hard to clear up or clean up after they've been said. I know I need to come clean.

"Are you going to tell me or are you trying hard to make up a lie?"

I look her straight in the eye. "I will *never* lie to you and I would *never* cheat on you. But what I say may make you hate me." She draws her eyebrows together, thinking.

I sit back in my seat waiting on her to open the door and run, but she doesn't. Continuing, I say, "All I ask is that you hear me out before you try to leave."

She nods, "Okay, I promise.

"When Cain and I were little, I was always the troublemaker." She snorts. I point to my chest. "I know it seemed like it was always me, but half the time it was actually Cain doing stupid stuff. He painted the school columns using profanity. Do you remember that?"

"Yes! But that was you?"

"Everyone thought it was me. Shit, we were identical, but it wasn't me. But I'm the one who got in trouble for it."

"Why didn't you tell the principal it was Cain?" she asks, assuming I had never tried telling our teachers, parents, or the chief of police it wasn't me. It also wasn't me who let out Floyd's cows from his pasture. Those damn things roamed the town on Haydenville Day but no one believed me. They all believed it was true when Floyd's wife pointed at me and said *it was him. He's the one that let out the cows.*

"Cain made himself out to be the golden boy. The one that never did anything wrong. He loved all the attention, the praise he got from all the adults." I shake my head remembering all the crap I got in trouble for. "When we were younger we were really competitive, but as we grew older he became destructive." She doesn't say anything. "I did my best to stay away from him, but when he saw the way I looked at you... The day you bumped into me in the hallway was a enlightening moment. I'll never forget how you smelled. From then on even the smallest brush up against you made my insides light up with electricity running through my veins."

"I thought it was Cain that I bumped into." She looks more confused.

"Did he tell you that?"

She pauses for a long moment. "Yes... he came up to me shortly after I bumped into... you. Hmm." She stops talking, rubs her forehead and then she throws her hands up in the air. "This is all too confusing. Why would he do that? Why would he pretend to be the guy I bumped into?" Her eyes are filled with sorrow. Everything I've dumped on her, plus finding out about Cain's infidelity, is more than one person should have to take.

"He did it because I wanted you, and he wanted to challenge me to see who could get you. When I told him no, he didn't stop. Taking you away to make you love him was his revenge against me." I reach over to hold her hand. "I never meant to tell you this to hurt you. I don't want that. I just… I had to tell you how strongly I felt about you. How strongly I still feel about you." She lets me hold her hand while she's silent—only communicating with her eyes. They're flowing with tears of despair. Paige doesn't look at me or even blink her eyes. "Will you say something."

"I don't know what to say."

She hates me.

"Do you still want to have dinner?" Pushing her would be a bad choice but I could just tie her up until she's ready to talk to me. Angrily lashing out at me would be better than not speaking to me. At least we would be communicating even if it she was hitting me and I was enduring bodily harm.

My patience is rewarded when she finally gives me a nod. Taking it as a good sign, I do a mental dance.

"Stay right there."

CHAPTER TWENTY-FIVE

Cade

The hostess leads us to our table. Walking around Paige, I pull out her chair, silently asking for an olive branch. Lucky for me this woman has real class because she takes her seat and whispers a thank you.

Despite that, I'm beating myself up for telling Paige she was just part of a stupid challenge. There's no argument that Cain fell in love with her. I can see it in his eyes when I look at the pictures on the walls of the house they once shared.

"Can I get you something to drink?" The waiter hands us each a drink menu.

"I'll have a glass of water. What would you like to drink?" I ask Paige.

"Hmm, Chardonnay."

The waiter bends slightly at the waist, then walks to the bar.

"Can we please not talk about Cain tonight?" Paige asks in a small voice.

"That sounds like a great idea to me." I relax a little at her words.

Paige pops open her menu and studies it as if she's expecting a pop quiz at the end of the night.

I really fucked up. I was going to tell her everything, tell her that I was the one who crawled into her bedroom that night. But now is not a good time.

As Paige looks over the menu, I keep stealing glances at her, mesmerized by her beauty. Her skin looks so smooth, soft. All I want to do is hold her in my arms and rock my body into hers. My cock stirs, waking up from hibernation.

"Stop staring," she tells me without lifting her gaze from the menu.

"How do you know I'm staring?" I raise my eyebrows.

"I can feel you."

I want to feel you... up. I don't say it but it doesn't mean I don't want to do it.

"The way you're studying that menu, I may have to give you a test on it later," I joke.

"Hmm. That's because I want to make sure I order the most expensive thing on the menu. Since you're buying." She looks up at me. "You look like your pockets are deep."

I raise an eyebrow. "Really?" It's not a lie. I'm worth a million. You wouldn't know it by looking at me, though. I don't indulge in material items. The only luxury I've allowed myself to purchase is my car. The majority of my money is in investments or locked away in my safe.

"Your car is the same price as a small house," she says with a small curl of her lip.

"It's the only possession I have." I'm being honest. I've never bought a house. There's never been a Mrs. Cade, so I've been lucky enough to save my money.

"You mean you—" She lets her mouth drop open with her lips puckered. She looks adorable when she's speechless.

"Paige!" A voice from across the dining room interrupts us.

Pace weaves between the tables to hug her sister.

"Oh," Pace's head bounces between me and Paige. "I didn't know you two were having dinner."

"It's just dinner," Paige says.

It stings a little that it's *just dinner* to her. This means more to me than my damn car and I love that fucking thing.

"Who are you here with?" Paige asks Pace.

Pace's face goes all happy puppy dog. "Oh my god. I have got to tell you," she whispers.

"There you are. I didn't know where you went off to." *Fucking Dillion.* "Holy shit! Small world isn't it?" he says when he looks down at us.

Small world, my fucking ass. He planned this. Of all the women he could date or fuck he chooses Paige's sister. Someone who is way too young for him.

"Imagine that," I grit out.

Paige sits like a marble statue and is almost as pale. *Why is she so pale?*

"Babe, are you okay? You look like you've seen a ghost." She blinks once then twice.

"I need to use the restroom." She scrapes her chair back and stands up.

"I'll go with you," Pace tells Paige's back. Then she turns to her date. "Dillion, ask them to bring two more chairs. We can sit with Paige and Cade. Oh, I forgot to introduce you." Pace turns to where her sister has walked off. "Shit, I need to go check on her. Dillion. Cade. Cade. Dillion." She says it in a hurry before she rushes after Paige.

I sneer at Dillion. Waiting until Pace is out of sight, I bark, "What the fuck are you doing here with her?"

His demeanor is cool as he summons a waiter and asks, "Excuse me. Can you bring two more chairs for the table?"

When the chairs are brought over, he takes a seat in one of them, looking completely relaxed.

"Are you going to fucking answer me?"

"I'm on a date."

"With Paige's sister?" I clench my teeth tightly.

"Seems like it." He takes a sip of water from my glass. "Didn't realize they were sisters."

It's a lie, I'm sure, so I challenge him. "You didn't know." I squint my eyes at him. "That's highly unlikely. You not knowing who someone is, is bullshit. You forget, I know you better than anyone. I know that you can run background checks on anyone."

He throws his head back, laughing. I have the urge to stab him in the throat with the silverware in front of me.

"I'm actually quite fond of Pace. She's...a delight to be around."

"Oh great, they brought us chairs." Pace pulls out the empty chair while Paige takes her seat.

"Paige, are you feeling well?" I didn't miss how she got up and ran to the bathroom as soon as Dillion came up to the table.

"Mmhmm," she replies.

"Would you like to leave?" Finally, she looks up at me. Her eyes are wide. Dillion turns his head to look at her. I can't see his face but I can feel how uneasy Paige is. I throw my napkin down. "Let's go. Pace come on. I'm taking you home." Pace looks at me like I've lost my damn mind.

"Dillion is taking me home," she protests.

I lean over the table. "Will he? Do you really know him?" Her eyes fill with questions as they dart over to Dillion.

"What is he talking about?" she questions Dillion.

He shrugs his shoulders. "No idea."

"Let's go." My chair falls backwards when I stand quickly.

Dillion raises up but I push him back down in his chair by placing my hands on his shoulders.

"Don't. You sit your ass down and stay seated till we leave. Don't fucking follow us out."

I take a hold of Paige's hand. She closes her fingers around mine, letting me lead the way with Pace following behind. I hurry them to my car, then get Paige settled in the front seat and Pace in the back.

When I close my car door, I buckle up. As I pull out of the parking lot, I reach over to put Paige's hand on my thigh. "Is Pace still staying with you?" I ask Paige, who is staring straight ahead. She hasn't removed her hand from my thigh, though.

"Yes."

We drive in silence for a few minutes until I can't take it any longer.

"Talk to me." I look over at her. "Was it what I said earlier?"

She exhales. "I was surprised to see Pace walk in with him."

"Is there something else?"

"No."

I don't believe her. Something is off with how she's acting.

"Can somebody tell me what is going on? I'm right here, you know," Pace pleads from the back seat.

"When did you meet him?" Paige looks over her shoulder to ask Pace.

"Four days ago but we've been on the phone talking ever since. He's so hot!"

"Forget him," I tell her. "He's trouble. The kind you don't want to be involved with."

"Are you sure? Maybe you're mistaking him for someone else." I can hear the hope in Pace's voice.

"No. I'm serious. If you ever see him coming your way, walk the other way, and fast," I warn her as I pull into Paige's driveway.

"Damn, it's always the hot ones." She gets out of the car and heads inside the house.

I twist in my seat to look at Paige. "I know something is wrong. Tell me. I want to help."

Her hand is shaking as she reaches up to brush back the hair that's fallen in her face. "I saw Dillion at Hershall's gas station today."

My hand tightens on the steering wheel.

He followed her.

"Go on," I encourage her, surprised my voice doesn't betray my inner turmoil.

"Before I stopped to get gas, a Chevy SUV practically ran me off the road. Thank goodness that stretch of highway has a shoulder." She swallows. "He stopped at the gas station and came up to speak to me, and when he left, he waved to me from his vehicle. He was driving the same SUV that ran me off the road." Turning her head to look at me, she continues. "Cade, the children were with me. I know that you're into some shady stuff. Cain told me. But... I can't have that around my children. I won't let you bring that around them." A tear falls from the corner of her eye. Reaching over, I gently wipe it away.

"I'm not a part of that world anymore. I wouldn't have ever *been* a part of that world if it wasn't..." I trail off, not wanting to finish that sentence. It's best I leave out the past, not tell her how Cain blackmailed to force me to leave. "I've done some things but I've left that behind me. I want to start a new life. A life that includes you and the kids. I'm not going to let anyone hold me back. I want you, Paige. I've *always* wanted you."

My hand threads into her hair, pulling her closer. My lips touch hers and a spark zips though me. Never has anything felt so right. We kiss, open mouthed, tongues stroking, and it's everything I remember. Every small kiss I've been granted in the last few weeks has reminded me of how strong my love is for her.

When she pulls back, I want to pull her closer again but scaring her would destroy any progress I've made. So I allow her to have space. Just a moment before I take another taste of her lips.

"I'm opening my own security company. I went to see an investor today."

"Really?" There is excitement in her voice.

I smile and she smiles back. For the first time tonight, everything feels right.

"Yeah, I meant what I said. I'm not going to let anyone or anything keep me from you. Do you think you're ready to move on, give me a chance? You feel this connection too, I know you do."

"Yeah, I do. I'm…worried. What's your family going to think of us? Me being married to one brother and then dating his twin."

"Let me take care of that. This Sunday, bring the kids over to my parents' house. We'll have lunch and tell them about us. If they don't like it then we'll leave. But something tells me they won't be opposed to it."

Her smile gives me hope that everything is going to be okay. Once I get rid of Dillion.

CHAPTER TWENTY-SIX

Paige

"Are you sure?" Pace asks me again for the fifth time.

"Yes," I exclaim, getting frustrated that she doesn't believe me about Dillion.

"Why me? Why me? Every time I meet a good looking guy he turns out to be a jerk. Why didn't you tell me he's a bad guy?" She gives me a hard look.

I'm trying to wash clothes and clean the house, but I'm not having much luck with Pace following me from room to room. She's been asking me questions about last night's awkward events.

"It's not you. There just seem to be more bad guys than good guys out there. You're going to meet someone," I say to encourage her to not give up looking.

"That's easy for you to say. You had the same guy since high school. Now you've got another guy who adores you just as much as the first one."

My lips tingle, remembering the kiss we shared last night. It was soft and then hard when it needed to be. It made little fireflies flit along my body, lighting up all my girl parts. I haven't had my girl parts light up in so long.

"Oh, I know that look of happiness on your face," Pace exclaims. "Did you get a hotdog last night?" She bounces on her feet.

Ugh, I hate that she calls a man's penis a hotdog. She's done that since she was four, when she accidentally barged in while Dad was peeing. It was cute then but she's kept the term. Somehow it always manages to gross me out.

My phone beeps in my back pocket and I eagerly pull it out, hoping to see a message from Cade. No such luck.

"What's that face? Who is it?" Pace looks over my shoulder. "Is she still calling?"

It's Kellie. She's not let up with her constant text messages and calls. I know I need to put her out of her misery by answering the phone but I haven't had the strength to deal with her. Also, because I don't want to hear the many excuses she'll give me to justify an affair with my husband.

"Just face her. Meet her somewhere and if it's too much, get up and walk away."

She's right. I need to put an end to this. I don't want to have this conversation over the phone.

I send off a text telling her, *Can't talk, busy.*

She messages me back, *Can we please meet? I need to talk to you.*

Groaning, I toss my head back and close my eyes. She's the last person I want to hear from right now but Pace is right. I need to put a stop to the endless calls and messages.

I shoot her a text to let her know I'll be at The Brew House after work on Monday if she wants to meet. She replies that she'll be there and I groan louder than before, knowing I'm going to have to see her face to face.

Settling into a chair at The Brew House, I look out the

window and watch the traffic pass by. The coffee shop is located in the middle of our small town. It's owned by the Covingtons, who also own the flower shop next door. It's cute, with small tables and chairs in front of the counter. It even has a small patio outside where you can sit. I chose to stay inside today but select a table as far as possible from the front door. The last thing I want is for the town to be gossiping more about Cain's and my relationship.

Last week, when I was in a stall in the ladies' restroom at work, I overheard two women talking about Cain's infamous affair with Kellie. I wanted nothing more than for the earth to swallow me up. Mortified, I stayed in the stall until they left and then, to be doubly sure no one else was in the restroom, I stood on the toilet seat to look over the stall walls before I walked out to wash my hands.

Kellie walks in the coffee shop door and scans the room, seeking me out. Plastering a fake smile on, I sit up straighter.

She eases down in the chair across from me. "Thank you for meeting me."

I wrangle the words jumbled up in my throat and manage to speak. "Sure. What did you want to talk to me about?" My voice is harsh. What does she expect though? The affair she and Cain kept hidden from me was the worst betrayal one person can inflict on another.

Her voice is faint and the words she utters are unintelligible. I want to roll my eyes at her. Her innocent act is unbearable to watch.

"I really can't hear or understand anything you are saying." The bitch in me has come out with her nails extended, ready to rip into her for the hurt she's caused me.

She clears her throat. "I wanted to apologize… I know no matter how many times I say sorry it won't ever be enough."

"You're right. It won't." I stare at her. "Is that all you

wanted to say?" I give her an annoyed expression.

"No. I've told Kip that Cain was his father." She pauses.

Poor Kip. He's innocent and shouldn't have to be dragged through Cain and Kellie's shit. Kellie has no idea how she's smeared not just her name but Kip's. He'll have to listen to the whispers throughout town of what a whore his mother was.

She gives me her sad eyes. Well too fucking bad. I don't feel anything for her anymore, except disgust.

"Kip is so upset with me for not telling him. I'm at a loss here." She shakes her head and lifts her hands up to wipe her eyes. "He called my mother to come get him. My mother! My parents didn't even want to raise *me*. Now all of a sudden they want to take my son in." I stay quiet, hoping she'll hurry up and finish. "Are you going to say anything?" she begs.

Exhaling, I ask her, "What do you want me to say? What could I possibly say that would make everything better? Kellie, you only invited me here to feel sorry for you. You didn't invite me here to really apologize. You invited me here to listen to you complain about how the word finally got out that you fucked my husband, got knocked up, and finally, after years of keeping it a secret, you got caught." She gawks at me. "Did I get it right?" I take a sip of the coffee I ordered before she sat down.

The door swings open and I watch Cade walk up to the counter to order. Movement outside the window catches my eye and I see a black SUV parking across the street. Kellie starts talking again—I can see her lips move but I can't understand her. The sound of the cash register and the hiss of the espresso machine are loud in my ears, though.

"Paige, Paige." Kellie shakes my shoulder to wake me out of my trance.

I look around the shop, and Cade is watching me with his brows drawn together. I signal with my eyes to the window to make him aware of the SUV. He nods. That's when it dawns on me that he already knew. He'd come in to keep me safe.

"Yeah, I'm fine." I look out the window again, but a green minivan is now parked where the black SUV was. "I need to go." As I gather my things, Kellie places her hand out to stop me.

"Let me finish." I give her my attention and she goes on. "Earning your trust will be hard. I know this. I know I deserve whatever you want to dish out but please don't take it out on Kip. He wants to talk to you. He has questions about his father." I cringe at those words. *His father.* "I should have said it from the beginning. I guess... I was hoping you would forgive me."

"I'm not ready to discuss Cain right now." She looks defeated. A small tug pulls at my heart. "It's not Kip. I'm just not at a strong enough place to accept all that's happened."

I turn back to the cash register. Cade is still standing there, observing the activity in front of the coffee shop, like he's waiting for something to happen. How in the hell did I go from being a boring mom, teacher, and widow to dealing with a mistress and a man that I suspect is more dangerous than a stick of dynamite?

I return my attention to Kellie. "But when I get there, I'll give you a call. You can drop Kip off one day to play with the kids. I'll do my best to answer his questions. But please stop calling and messaging. I've got too much on my plate right now."

She must have felt more comfortable after our talk, because she agrees to wait till I call. I couldn't be more thankful for the space right now.

After she's left, Cade sits in her empty seat. "Did you work everything out?"

"It's going to take time." He bites his pastry and watching

his mouth makes my thighs clench.

"That's understandable." He speaks around a mouthful of cheese Danish.

Tires squeal and a scream follows. My heart races because I know that scream. A white van is stopped in front of the shop. The driver quickly reverses into a side street, then pulls out and speeds off, dodging something in the street on his way.

"Fuck!" Cade jumps up, racing outside and leaping over a planter to make it to the person laying on the pavement.

I stand in shock for a moment, then head outside. I take one slow step after another, using them to calm the ferocious beating of my heart. Cain looms over Kellie's still lifeless body. Blood pools around her, evidence that a life once exist in the shell it's draining from.

"Is she," I can't say the last word. I can't push enough air through my throat to speak. Tears don't stream down my face. There's nothing but guilt. I could have been nicer. I could have said I forgave her. But how could I have forgiven her when she did what she did?

Strong arms pull me into a hard body, anchoring me. I bury my face into a muscled chest.

Cade's voice is rougher than normal. "It's not your fault."

I peer up at him. When did being around him become like… home? His gray eyes are alert and attentive as they watch my face. I want nothing more than to drown in them.

"Why didn't they get out of the vehicle? Did they not see her?" My voice is full of worry.

"I don't know," is all he says.

Sirens wail around us. Men and women rush to Kellie but it's too late. She's gone. Nothing but a leather bag of human remains is left laying on the pavement.

"Excuse me, did either one of you see what happened?" a middle-age man asks. He's in a police uniform.

"No, we were having coffee with the victim. She left before us. We heard a scream but that was it. I came out and saw her laying on the road," Cade replies.

The officer's eyes scan across the area. "You didn't see a vehicle?" His eyes come back around to hold Cade's in a challenge.

"A white van." Cade squeezes me a little, giving me comfort.

"I saw it." An older woman yells out. She's sitting in a rocking chair in front of the drug store across from the coffee shop. "I saw everything." She keeps rocking. The officer shoots an exasperated facial expression in the woman's direction. "Poor thing, she just walked right in front of that van. Even looked before she stepped down from the sidewalk. I'd say she did it on purpose."

My jaw plummets. *No, she wouldn't.* I know she was upset that Kip went to his grandparents but it would have passed. There was no need to take her own life.

I stand off to the side while Cade talks to the officer. The coroner loads up Kellie's body and it hits me that Kip will be told shortly about his mother dying. He's so young. Kellie was right. Her parents were not the best at raising her. They don't deserve to raise Kip or any child. Maybe it would be best if I check in on him.

CHAPTER TWENTY-SEVEN

Paige

The next few days are more familiar than I care to remember. They bring up memories of burying Cain. Memories that I've been trying my best to put behind me.

Kellie's service was well attended. Not surprising, since she grew up here and had a successful salon. Her parents sat in the front row, but there was no sign of Kip, which struck me as odd. But I was too wrapped up in Cade's presence beside me, in keeping my own children still and quiet, and in my memories to dwell on it.

After the service for Kellie, her mother asked me to join the family at the law office of Jose Burns. I can't imagine why they asked me to go. Kellie and I have no ties other than our years of so-called friendship.

"Are you headed to the law office now?" Cade asks.

"No, the meeting is after lunch, so I want to take the kids to the Burger Shack first. My parents are still in town, so I'll drop them off to stay with them while I head to the lawyer's office."

"Any idea what it's about?" he asks.

"No. Not really. I'm surprised I was invited." I look

around and then whisper, "Have you seen Dillion?"

"Fucker is staying out of sight. I have no idea where he's at."

"Thank you for coming with the kids and me." He wraps his arm around my shoulders, pulling me in.

Kissing the top of my head, he asks, "Mind if I crash the party at the Burger Shack?"

My heart skips. "Not at all."

"Good because I was coming anyway." His voice is light and playful.

Images of Cade as a teenager flash through my mind. His charismatic charm used to make all the girls swoon. I was one of them.

Shaking myself out of my thoughts, we gather the children and head to the restaurant. While Cade places our order, I choose the booth and the kids scramble off to the adjoining indoor play area while we wait.

Cade struts over to the booth and slides in beside me. We sit closer than normal. Our thighs touch. I can't say I hate it. It actually feels nice being close to him. Every small touch I get from him makes me feel wanted.

It's funny how I never truly felt that I was everything Cain wanted. The more I look back on our relationship, I see things I'd missed before. I see now those moments that should have led me to discover the affair. All the late night runs and work meetings, how we made love less and less. How he kept his phone locked and wouldn't give me the code when I asked for it. I remember the time, when we were sitting at a red light… I didn't have my phone with me and wanted to check on the weather for Ivory's field trip to the zoo the next day. I grabbed his phone and asked for the passcode Cain yanked it from my hand to enter it himself. I should have suspected something then but I brushed it off.

Now with both of them gone, I guess I'll never find out

more than what I already know. I'll never get to ask him if he ever truly loved me. Was I just a stupid challenge to him? I've had to mentally prepare myself to let go, bury it. To follow Julia's advice to bury the past and move on, to not dig it back up because skeletons are all that lie there. Today… I did it. Deciding it would be best to bury the past with Kellie, I left it for the grave diggers to cover it over with dirt as they covered Kellie's casket.

When the food arrived, Cain moved to sit opposite to me, so Jameson could sit next to me in a booster seat. He's leaning back now, puffing his stomach out to show how full he is. I push my finger into his belly making him laugh.

"Mommy." His sweet voice is playful.

"What?" I play innocent.

His short chubby finger pokes me in the boob, making Cade and Ivory laugh from their seats across the booth.

"Hey now. That's not my tummy." I rub my boob.

He laughs. The sound is sweeter than honey.

"Okay, is everyone done?" Ivory nods, Jameson is still poking his stomach out and Cade is sitting back watching the interaction with loving eyes. I put everyone's garbage on the tray to dump, taking glances up at Cade as I do. His eyes sweep over my face and land on my lips. I'm so distracted that I set trash down in Jameson's lap.

"Mommy!" he scolds me.

"Oh! I'm sorry, baby." I hurry to pick up a napkin to wipe the ketchup that smeared on his pants.

"It's okay. Even mommies make mistakes." His small hand pats me on the arm.

"Why don't I take the kids to your parents?" Cade offers. "Then I'll meet you at the lawyer's office."

I'm a little stunned he offered. That's so sweet of him. With Cain, I always did all the car pooling, taking the kids anywhere they needed to go.

"That would be nice." I blink, looking between the kids. "Would you guys be okay to ride with Cade to Nana's and Paw Paw's?"

They both jump in their seats with excitement.

I mouth a thank you to Cade. He gives a nod, appearing to be just as pleased as the children are.

When I pull up at the lawyer's office, I notice Kellie's parents' empty car parked in front. Hurrying as fast as possible, I burst through the front double doors. A woman in her mid-thirties is sitting at a large wooden desk.

"Ms. Staton?" She says my name but it's more of a question.

"Yes, that's me."

"Come with me." She leads me down a hallway that's lined with large portraits. Although they are of different men, somehow they all have the same facial features. Large, sloping noses, round eyes and thin lips. There's no denying those men are relatives from several generations.

"Here you go. Everyone is already seated." She opens the door. The office has ceiling-to-floor bookcases that line the walls on either side of the desk. They are packed with row after row of books of different sizes. *I don't suppose any of them are romance novels.*

My shoulder brushes up against the door and a sharp pain hits me like a bolt of lighting in my gut. I recognize Mr. Burns from seeing him in the community, and the wrinkles at his eyes have more depth in them when he greets me with a genuine smile.

"Ms. Staton." He is seated behind his desk, but stands to greet me. "So glad you were able to join us. Please have a seat." He gestures to a brown leather chair parked in front of his desk. Kellie's parents are seated on a loveseat off to the right, next to a large window.

"Thank you."

When he takes his seat, he glances down at some papers, then back up to address us. "This appears to be everyone. There's not much in the will, everything is going to Kip Young, who is a minor."

Mr. Burns rattles on, following the standard procedure of reading Kellie's will and testament. My mind wanders as I sit there.

"Will go to Ms. Staton." Hearing my name jerks me back to the present.

"I'm sorry. What did you say?" Mrs. Young's voice is full of bitterness.

Mr. Young sits there like he's bored, but Mrs. Young extends her fangs, ready to attack.

"The will states that guardianship of Kip Douglas Young resides with you, Ms. Staton."

Douglas, Cain's middle name. All the signs were there, and I missed them. What a fool I was.

"But I'm not a relative." The words stumble out.

"That's right. We're..." Mrs. Young hooks her thumb between her and Mr. Young. "We're her parents. Don't we have any rights?" Her voice is full of irritation.

"Regardless, the will states that first choice of guardianship is Cain Staton, who is deceased. Second is Paige Staton." He points to me, his voice firm.

Me? Why me?

My body slumps backwards in the chair. Can I really take care of Cain and Kellie's love child? Can I treat him as an equal to my own children? I don't think I can. It would break me every time I looked at him. Wouldn't it?

"Ms. Staton, do you accept the responsibility?"

Digging deep, my mouth falls open to answer but I'm left

without words.

A small creaking noise comes from behind me. We all turn to see an unkempt child walk in. A wave of guilt slaps me in the face. His face, hair, and clothes are dirty, like he hasn't had a bath in days. The clothes are not his because they overwhelm his small frame. Holes as big as my fist are torn in them.

Entering the room, he walks at a snail's pace. As if he's afraid of getting bitten. The happy beaming gray eyes I remember are dull, lifeless. It only takes one look at him to know what I need to do. What I must do.

CHAPTER TWENTY-EIGHT
Paige

Walking hand in hand, Kip and I leave the room that's now filled with air made toxic by the vitriol of Mr. and Mrs. Young. I couldn't sign the papers fast enough to leave. To free Kip from the suffocating hold that Kellie had to endure as she grew up in their house.

Cade stands by the front door of the building, staring out the window as he waits for us. Seeing him ignites butterflies dancing up my spine. His large frame is outlined by the sun beaming through the window. The man oozes danger—all those tattoos peaking out of his collar and swirling around his arms. His profile shows the hard set of his face.

"Cade." I touch his shoulder causing him to jerk back, drawing his arm up.

Kip gasps next to me, throwing his arm over his head. My heart melts. *Did Kellie's parents abuse him?*

"Kip," my whole attention focuses on him. "It's okay." I pull him against me. This little boy may be the outcome of an affair but he doesn't deserve to be abused, used for capital gain. Mr. and Mrs. Young saw him as an asset, a way for them to have access to any money Kellie had. They've always been the kind of people who expected a handout.

Cade winces at Kip's fright. I give him wide eyes privately, asking him to comfort Kip.

Bending at his knees, Cade gets down to Kip's level. "Hey," he touches Kip's shoulder, trying to get Kip to face him. "I didn't mean to startle you. I was taken by surprise, that's all." Cade looks up to me, helpless. The strong beast never looked more sexy. My body buzzes with the need to shower him with kisses. To show him how he truly makes me feel inside.

Kip stays planted at my side. His small arms are wrapped around my middle. Turning my eyes down to him, I use a soft tone to ease his worry. "Let's go get Jameson and Ivory. We'll pick them up, go home, get comfy, and veg out on the couch. Does that sound like fun?" I give him a big smile. Trying to encourage him, I add more sweetness to the deal. "We'll let you pick out the movie!"

Kip perks up a hair then settles his eyes back on his feet. I hold him close to me as we walk out. Once he's loaded in my SUV, Cade pulls me back out of hearing range from Kip.

"What the hell." His voice is a little too loud.

"Shh," I look through the window to see if Kip is listening. When I see he's not, I offer up an explanation to Cade.

"Kellie left guardianship to Cain and me." I rub my face in my palms. "I'm sure she never thought something would happen," I whisper so low I can barely hear myself. "Or that she would commit suicide because that's what it seems she did. She committed suicide not even thinking about that little boy." I point my finger in Kip's direction, letting my behavior become enraged. "You saw him. That's not the same carefree little boy who was at Ivory's birthday party. That's a boy that's been thrown to two devious human beings that only want him for a government check and access to his mother's money." I inhale and exhale, trying to steal myself. "I couldn't say no when I saw him walk in. They didn't even bother to clean him up. They could have at least made it look like they cared."

Cade nods, understanding that Kip couldn't go back to those horrible people. I couldn't do that to an innocent soul. Sending him to the wolves without anyone protecting him, there's no way I could do that.

"Do you want me to go pick up the children, meet you back at your place?" he offers.

My eyes wander over to his shiny sports car. He must have swung by his parents' house, dropped off his dad's truck and retrieved his car.

"Where would they fit?" I ask playfully.

"There's a backseat." He pretends hurt at my question.

I shake my head. "I think..." I look at the back seat where Kip's sitting. A large sigh comes out. "I think it'll do Kip good, start the healing process, if he sees Ivory and Jameson being excited to see him. Maybe it will lift his spirits a bit."

Cade kisses my forehead and promises to come over in an hour, letting me know he needs to run an errand before he comes over.

"Hopefully, it won't take long."

Before he pulls back, I inhale his scent. I let the smell of him, cedarwood and rainforest, invade my lungs. It calms my anxiety about what I'm about to undertake. Am I doing the right thing by taking Kip into my home? Can I give him the same love I give my own children? I pray to God above for the strength to stitch up all the wounds that Cain and Kellie have inflicted, so I can give Kip the love he's rightfully due.

An hour later, the children are laying on an assortment of blankets and pillows, piled high on the living room floor. All three are snuggled together as if this is an everyday movie night. My heart hums at the sight of Kip in the middle of Ivory and Jameson. He's every bit of a big brother to them even if we didn't know he actually was.

Jameson and Ivory were overcome with happiness when Kip walked in at my parents' house. I couldn't stop the warm feeling that spread through me when they both ran to him with arms wide open, squeezing him as if he were a life line.

Kip tips his head back, "Are you coming to sit with us, Ms. Paige?"

I'm standing at the window, scanning the driveway for any sign of Cade. Apprehension is gnawing at my bones—worry that something has happened. It's been over an hour without any word from Cade. No messages, no calls. I've been pacing the floor, watching the driveway, waiting for him to pull up.

Cade has been spending more time with us, and I've become used to him being a fixture in our home. The Sunday we spent with his folks was just like any other Sunday afternoon. We laughed, played with the kids, and ate dinner. Except this time, Cade had announced that he loved me. The table went silent at his declaration. I had been so worried about what they would say, but his mother laughed, throwing me off guard. She'd already known. She could see it in her son's eyes. Then each one around the table laughed and congratulated us, and wished us happiness. I couldn't believe it. I had been so nervous… over nothing.

Giving Kip a faint smile, I reply, "I'm coming," then I take one more long gaze out the window, silently saying a prayer that he's safe.

When the movie ends, I lift up off the couch. All three

children are asleep in a pile on their pallet. The clock on the wall opposite me reads ten. Still no word from Cade and it's been hours, since that was our second movie. Just as I accept that I won't hear from him tonight, right then my phone starts buzzing on the coffee table. Quickly I scrambled to reach it, hoping, praying it's him and he's okay. I fumble to hit the green button and almost drop it onto the hard floor. Cade's name is stretched across the screen.

"Oh god, Cade." The gust of air leaves my throat so fast I almost don't register what I've said. "Are you okay? Where are you?" My questions come out in a hurry. I want to wave a magic wand and make him appear beside me.

His voice is rough when he speaks, "I'm okay." The way he says it doesn't convince me.

"Are you on your way here?" I want to see him. Check him for any bodily harm. My need to be around him has grown by leaps and bounds in the past couple of weeks. He's somehow inched his way into our lives... and my heart.

"No, I'm not going to make it tonight. I've had some... things come up. I'll call you tomorrow."

"Will you come over tomorrow?" My insides quake with an uneasy feeling.

He's doing another job. A job that could cause him harm.

"I'm out of town but when I get back, I want to talk." His voice is firm.

My chest rises and falls with my rapid heartbeats. I can't do this. I can't be that type of woman who stays at home while he goes off and does who knows what. Didn't he tell me he was going clean?

"Sure." I barely whisper it into the phone. I want to ask a million questions, but I decide not to. Cain used to hate it when I asked questions.

"Babe," he says, his voice low. "Don't. Don't let that pretty mind start to worry. I'm not going to let anything or anyone come between us. I'll explain everything when I see you again. Please understand."

"Yeah, understood." I want to believe him. But how can I when he doesn't want to tell me anything. Maybe this is all for the best. I have more responsibilities now with Kip living here with us.

CHAPTER TWENTY-NINE

Cade

I growl out loud. I've never wanted to rip someone apart as badly as I do right this moment.

"You'll thank me." Dillion says from the leather seat of my car. "You wouldn't want what happened to dear sweet Kellie to happen to Paige... would you?" His grin is wild, sinful, leaving me to wonder how I didn't see his thirst for money and havoc right from the start.

My skin feels itchy, like a fire is burning below its the outer layer, ready to be rid of Dillion once and for all.

"Last job," I confirm.

"Sure, until the next one. Come on. You love it just as much as I do." He tilts his head. "You think she's going to be able to make a man like you happy?" He pauses. Shaking his head he says, "Men like us don't live the happy ever after. Men like us live in dark dreams causing pain for others."

This time I shake my head, trying to expel the nightmares I've lived through. I don't need to go back and dig up those haunted memories. Inflicting pain on men and women was to tip the scales so that good would win. It wasn't to tip the scale of my bank account.

"Speak for yourself." My voice is full of malice. I want to live that life. The one that I've dreamed of for so many years. Being with Paige. Now is my chance.

Laughing, Dillion throws a brown envelope in my lap. "All the details are in it. Who, where, and how they want it done. Your half of the deposit is also included." He opens the door and sticks a foot outside before he turns back. "Don't be an idiot. Do the job." He climbs all the way out and shuts his door.

When he's finally gone, I breathe a little better without his venom in the air, poisoning my insides with every breath I take. Picking up the envelope, I open it and study the pictures and documents. The photo shows a man in his late thirties holding a boy who's close to Jameson's age. In the photo he appears to be a doting father. The documents are his everyday routine, where he works, his home address, and what days his kid has baseball practice. Everything I'll need to study to make my move.

In with all the documents is a small envelope. Opening it, I find a plane ticket neatly tucked inside. Canada. *Fuck!* If that wasn't bad enough, I fly out in two hours. Which doesn't give me time to see Paige. Glancing at my watch, I curse again. I was supposed to be there hours ago. Dillion had called while Paige was in the lawyer's office saying he needed to see me, wanted to talk things out because he knew everything had gotten out of hand.

Fucker told me he had sent a warning, a white van. It didn't take me long to realize he was talking about Kellie. She was hit by a white van. His malicious words hit as hard as a brick to my gut. How he could do such a baleful act to an innocent woman, I'll never understand.

I thought I knew him better than anyone, but it turns out I was wrong, so fucking wrong.

A knock occurs at my driver's side window. Fucking

Dillion is standing there motioning me to roll the window down. Bending at the knees, he looks at me.

"You need to get going, Loverboy. Wouldn't want you to miss your flight." A crazy fucked up smile covers his face. "I'll make sure Paige is kept company."

I grab the handle on the door, ready to do battle. The door opens an inch before Dillion slams it back shut.

"Get going," he bellows out.

"Or what?" I challenge him with all the hatred I can muster up. Because right now I hate him. How did we become friends? He's more like Cain, always out for himself.

"Or you will have something to worry about."

"Touch her, touch anyone in her family, and I'll kill you… slow… and I'll enjoy the cries that'll come out of you. Feeding on them as if they were the best dessert I've ever had." This time his face pales.

That gives me a perverse comfort as I drive away. He knows I'll make good on my promise to him. I've taken a measure of joy in harming my victims. He's watched me, seen me take pleasure in others' pain. Performing procedures on them like we were in a dirty underground clinic. The only difference is, my victims weren't there by choice.

When my plane lands in Canada, I grab my rental car and head to the address in the file. It's an hour drive from the airport and that gives me plenty of time to think about what in the hell I'm going to do about Dillion.

Regret washes over me in waves. The life that I once lived, and then the life that my own brother—the bastard pushed me into. My anger re-ignites, this time as large sheets of fire covering my entire body. Cain. If it hadn't been for him, I wouldn't have had turn to a life that I'll never be able to escape. Dillion is going to trap me, use me for his gain. Being with Paige will always be a fantasy. A sweet experience only appearing in my daydreams since my nightmares haunt me at night, reminding me of who I have become.

Pulling up in front of the mark's house, I stop the car to study it. I scan the area, then I park next to the sidewalk and make my way to the back. I pick the lock and gradually open the door little by little. There's an alarm on the wall of the entryway. Taking wide steps I punch in the code, disengaging the alarm. I close the door and start to make my rounds in the house. I have all the information I need, but I like to do my own investigation, making sure nothing is missed. What rooms are connected to each other. Where the motion detectors are, if there is another keypad in any of the other rooms.

I pass by a picture in the hallway. An older man is holding onto the same small boy who is in the picture I have. But there's another boy standing beside him. He's looking up at the man with adoring eyes. Eyes that don't look haunted by abuse. Picking up the frame, I look at it closer. There's something familiar about the boy. His eyes and nose look just like... Dillion.

"What the fuck!"

A door slams from downstairs and I set the picture back just like it was. Creeping to the top of the stairs, I listen to what sounds like someone moving in the kitchen.

"Hey, is it set?" A woman's voice bounces up the stairs.

"What do you mean? I'm calling you to make sure it's a done deal." She's still for a moment. "Dillion," she hisses before I hear the sound of a phone dropping onto a hard surface. "Fucker," she says as her steps come closer.

I open a door. Stuffed animals line the head of a small bed. Toys are spread out on the floor, barely leaving any space to walk without tromping on them. Stepping inside, I open another door. It's a closet.

The footsteps stop outside the bedroom I'm in and I duck

into the closet, closing it just as the bedroom door opens.

The woman is ranting about her phone call. "Fucking idiot. He's so stupid he can't even tie his own damn shoe laces. He better get it done or no pussy for him. I'm sick of all this." Muffled noises from toys being thrown cut through the thin door. "Why in the hell can't this boy clean up. Ugh."

Another slam of a door from downstairs comes though the floor. Then small feet paddle their way upstairs.

"Hey Mom!" The voice from one of the sons greets her.

"Baby." The oversweetness of her voice makes me sick. "Did you have a good day?"

"Yeah, look what Dad got me." The boy must be holding up something to show her. She just grunts.

"Go get washed up and I'll be down in a little bit. Did your dad get the pizzas?"

"Yeah, he got your favorite. Cheese."

"Great, go on. I'll be there in a few."

After the boy leaves, I listen to heavy breathing and sighing from the conniving woman for what seems like an eternity before she finally exits the room.

"Fuck me. I didn't think she would ever leave," I whisper to myself.

I hear the family moving around below me. The mother yells out for the kids to grab their coats. Little feet start pounding on the stairs on the opposite side of the wall and I stand still, hoping the son who sleeps in this room won't come in.

When the door opens to the room I'm in, I close my eyes and hold my breath.

"Come on, Stanley. We have to go. Mom said no playing." The door shuts and I let out a gust of wind, deflating my chest.

Hurting children is not on my resume. I don't want to even be in a position like I'm in right fucking now. A position where a child will see me. The family was supposed to be gone till six. That's what Dillion's information said. Fucking Dillion.

Once I'm confident the family has left, I leave the house, finding my way back to my rental car. I stare at the house and decide to do a little research of my own. If Dillion had a call in for this man, Tommy would know.

Tommy's our contact at the Domestic Abuse Center. He's the heart of the operation. He's also a victim, not of sexual abuse, but physical abuse was an everyday occurrence for him growing up. He was determined to help others so they wouldn't have to go through what he did.

Tommy answers on the first ring. "Yo man."

"Tommy, how are you?" I haven't talked to Tommy in over a year. Not since I've been back home.

"I should be asking you that question. You just disappeared right off the edge of a cliff," he jokes.

"Yeah well, shit happens." I'm not going to tell everyone that a woman has got me so tied up in her hands that I'm barely breathing when she's not around.

"I heard that shit was a woman." Well, fuck!

"Dillion told you, huh?"

"Oh yeah. A drunk Dillion confesses everything. Especially, a drunk pissed Dillion. I say congratulations. You deserve it."

"Thanks, Tommy." I take a moment, gathering my nerve to ask.

I've never not trusted Dillion, but there's something here that doesn't add up. The woman's behavior was off. A woman that's being abused or aware of her children being abused doesn't act like a total bitch. I know what a total bitch acts like and that woman was it.

"Listen, I need a favor and I need it to stay between us."

"Sure thing. Anything for you."

I know he means it. Dude has had my back more times than I can count. His information has never led me wrong.

"Did you get a job for a…" I pick up the paper with the man's name. "Colson McDonald."

"Colson McDonald?" he repeats.

"Yeah." I spit out his address, hoping that will jog his memory.

"Fuck!" He sounds short winded.

"What the hell does that mean?" I question him.

"Fucking hell, Cade. That's Dillion's half-brother." Dumbfounded, I drop my head back to the headrest.

"Why in the hell would he put a hit on him? Why didn't he outsource?"

"That's a question for the insane man himself," Tommy chokes out. "Abort mission and find out what the hell is going through his head, ordering something on family. That's a risk we don't take. He knows we outsource that shit."

"Thanks, man. I'll be in contact."

"You better be."

Hanging up, I look at the house once more. I knew the oldest boy had the same eyes and nose as Dillion. "What are you up to Dillion?"

CHAPTER THIRTY
Paige

It's our first morning as a family of four. I've gotten the kids up, lunches are packed, and I'm making them a quick breakfast before we leave. This morning wasn't too bad. Just a few bumps getting Jameson up to get dressed—nothing unusual.

"Is Kip going to stay with us?" Ivory starts in on her twenty questions before my second cup of coffee.

"Yes, he going to live with us. Are you okay with that?" I watch her while I spread jam on her toast. Jameson and Kip are in the room they'll be sharing, putting on their shoes.

"Yeah, he's like Jameson but bigger."

More ways than one.

"Yep, he is." I grin, not knowing how to fit into the conversation that he's their half brother. Maybe, I should just rip off the bandage. Just tell them. They're so young. Would they know what I'm saying?

Both boys come barreling down the hallway, laughing and smiling, giving my heart a hard tug. *Okay heart, I know, I need to tell them.* When they take their seats at the bar, I place their toast and eggs on their plates.

Here goes nothing.

All three kids start digging into the food like starved little monkeys. I pour my second cup of pick-me-up and stand at the sink, watching them.

"What would you say if I told you that Kip is going to live with us permanently?"

Ivory speaks first. "I don't have to share my room with him, do I?" she whines.

"No, he'll be sharing Jameson's room with him." I tell her that as if it's a matter of fact.

"Jameson, what do you think?"

"Cool." One word to sum up his feelings.

That's my boy. Easygoing.

"Well, I have something else to tell you." Kip blinks up at me. His sweet face stiffens with fear. I reach across and place my hand on his, trying to reassure him that everything is going to be okay. "Kip is your half brother. Do you know what that means?"

Ivory stops and looks at me, pushing her eyebrows to the sky. "Did you have another baby?" she asks as she pulls her eyebrows back down and scrunches them together.

I give a gentle shake of my head.

"No, your daddy and Ms. Kellie had Kip when they were really young."

Jameson sits in his booster seat scraping up the last of his eggs while another twenty questions come out of Ivory. Always the inquisitive one—thank goodness these are easy questions. Then out of nowhere Ivory nails my feet to the floor with a question that comes out of left field. Although I should have known it was coming, with as much time as Cade has been spending with us.

"Are you going to marry Cade and have more babies?"

I spray my coffee out over the counter.

"I'm... not sure," I manage to say. Because I'm not. I

haven't even considered having more children or even marrying again. I feel like I'm still healing from the wounds caused by Cain. And who knows where the hell Cade is.

"If you do, can I name the baby?" Ivory pleads.

"No!" Jameson yells. "I want to name the baby."

Kip and I look at each other, grinning at the argument between Jameson and Ivory. I think that, if things do work out with Cade, I just might want another baby, because this feeling of the house being filled with laughter and fussing over the craziest things, heals all the holes in my heart.

It's been two days since Cade called me. He'd told me then that he would call me the next day, but he never did. My heart and mind are conflicted—I'm pissed and scared. Pissed because if he's okay, then he's not bothered to call and scared because what if something has happened to him.

Putting the last of the tests to be graded in my bag, I flick off the light to my classroom and leave the school. I casually stroll out to my car, bidding goodbye to the staff I see on my way. Pace picked up all three of the wild animals and she's preparing dinner at her house, my parents' house. They went back to Florida yesterday and I miss them already.

I'm about to open the back passenger door on the driver's side to drop off my bag, when my phone rings from my purse. Pulling it out, Cade's name flashes at the top. Anger surges through my hand, vibrating through my fingertips.

"You better have a good reason why you haven't called me," I explode.

"I'm waiting on you in your driveway. Come home and I'll explain everything." He hangs up, not giving me a chance to erupt on him. Which is a shame, because I've been laying awake at night dreaming of giving him a piece of my mind. If he wants my trust, he's going to have to do better than leading me around on a string, feeding me breadcrumbs.

Minutes later I'm pulling into the garage as a very pissed off Cade walks though the open door. His jaw ticks like he's grinding his back molars down to the nerves. His chest is puffed out, and he looks ready to pound on something. Even though he looks scary as hell, I'm completely turned on. And furious.

Pushing the remote on my sun visor, the garage door starts to close, casting a dark cloud over the thunderstorm brewing in the garage.

My rage wins, and as I get out of the car I round on him.

"Why did you wait until now to call me?" I yell. He's standing in front of me, sliding his hands in and out of his pockets. "Do you know how worried I was?" He's still silent. I throw my hands up, aggravated at his composure.

"Are the kids with you?" He bends to peer in the back windows.

"Pace has them at her house."

He straightens, his arm whips up and around my neck and he pulls me to him with a strong, powerful force. I don't have time to react before his lips take mine in a greedy attack. Sucking and licking, he bites his way down my neck while his free hand roams my side before he clutches my hip.

I moan at his assault. My hands drop my purse, and I hear the contents spill out and roll across the concrete floor. I press my palms to his chest, loving how hard it is.

One hand is still wrapped around my neck while the other one moves from my hip up to squeeze my breast, then back down over my hip and around to my ass. Grabbing a handful of my butt, he palms it, squeezing and kneading my ass. A growl travels up from the depths of his throat as desire shreds into him.

My skin is hot, sweaty, and sticky with the fierce need blazing inside of me. When he lowers both hands to the back of my thighs and lifts, I wrap my legs around his waist and pray this is not a dream.

In two steps he has me smashed up against the car, pinned in place by his hard body. I tug, pull, and claw at his t-shirt, lifting it over his head and throwing it, not caring where it lands.

His mouth makes its way back to mine and he murmurs, "Do you want my cock, baby?"

I moan as his tongue licks me, sending tingles straight to my core. The heat of his body is sending me to hell for all my immoral thoughts. In a quick movement, my shirt is lifted and tossed in the same manner as I just tossed his.

He pulls back and I lace my fingers through his short hair and pull him back to me, crashing our lips together. When he takes my bottom lip between his teeth, I whisper, "I want you so deep in me, pounding inside of me so hard, I'll be able to feel you for days."

He tilts his head up at the ceiling. "Fuck, I've been dreaming of this moment."

"Then take me, use my body, show me what should have been."

His eyes are filled with hunger as he reaches around and, with one flick, my bra is undone and the straps slide slid off my shoulders. He puts me down on the floor and pulls at the button on my slacks. His fingers unzip my pants, then push them down my hips. They pool at my feet. He steps back to assess me. His blue eyes are dark, raking over me—he's hungry and I am the feast.

"Fuck," he draws the word out. "You're not wearing panties."

I grin, "I hate panty lines."

A deep growl leaves his throat.

CHAPTER THIRTY-ONE
Cade

Here I stand, in front of Paige, aching for my cock to be planted inside her, pouring my seed into that sweet slick cunt. My cock is so engorged it's tenting my tight jeans. As I press my palm over the buttons of my jeans, trying to ease the throbbing in my cock, my eyes travel over Paige's body scorching her smooth skin. Smoke rises, sending my mind into a haze.

"You're perfect." The words fall effortlessly from my mouth.

Her pink cheeks deepen to a red.

A silent *thank you* breathes from between her lips.

Her perfect tits are taunting me, making my palms itch. Reaching up, I cup those luscious tits in my hands and bend forward to pull one to my mouth. Her nipple is hard and when I give it a long, wet lick, it almost slices through my damn tongue.

"Oh," she moans.

"Feel good, baby?" My voice is deep.

My throat is stuffed full with lust for this woman.

I grab the back of her thighs again and hoist her up. Her

legs wrap back around my waist and that sweet wet cunt rubs against my lower abdomen just above my low-slung jeans. Those perfect tits are now level with my face, and it's as if they demand that I open my mouth, latch onto one and suck. A deep growl in my throat vibrates the hard pebble. I gently clamp my teeth around it. I let my teeth scape the flesh as I pull my mouth away.

Her head is thrown back, and pleasure softens her features.

"I'm going to fill you so full with my cock." I wrap my arm around her waist to hold her against me. My other wraps under her peachy ass as I walk us into her house and to her bedroom.

I move my hand from under her ass until my index finger is rubbing through her lips, teasing her. She's so fucking wet. I pulse two fingers a knuckle deep in and out of her entrance.

"Fuck me. This little pussy is going to strangle the life out of my dick." I hum. "Me and Cain may have been identical twins, but there's one area that didn't get cut from the same mold." I grin.

Her cheeks burn with a deeper shade of red.

When I enter the bedroom, I walk over to the bed and throw her on top of it. She bounces on the mattress, a yelp escaping her mouth. I make quick work of unbuttoning my jeans and I push them down, taking my briefs too. My cock bobs toward Paige. Her eyes go wide at the sight of it. I grip my cock at the base, stroking myself, root to tip.

"Spread those legs, I want to see that pretty pussy." My eyes never leave Paige's drenched cunt. "I've got to be inside of you. Think you can take me, baby?"

"I want every inch filling me up, making me come undone."

"No barriers. I want to feel you." I've waited too long to

be with her again. The thought of anything between us is unbearable. "I'm clean, never been with anyone without being wrapped."

Not even you.

I already know Paige's history, no need to ask. Just giving her confirmation I'm clean. She must feel the need to confirm what I already know.

"I'm clean," she says in a low whisper.

Crawling on the bed, I climb onto her, supporting my weight on my elbows.

"There's no turning back. You're mine and no one else's." I reach between us, angling myself at her entrance. Her pussy is completely soaked.

The head of my cock edges her entrance. When I push in, I close my eyes.

"Fuckk," I groan. She feels too good. Too damn good. My jaws clench and I use all my strength to control my movements.

This beautiful, sweet woman under me deserves to be caressed, cherished. I plan on doing exactly that.

"Are you okay?" I ask as I try to push in a little more.

Paige's nails tear layers of flesh off my biceps. "I'm good." She's barely able to speak.

"I'm taking it as slow as I can, baby." I ease back out as I kiss her jaw. When I push further in, I still myself, giving my girl time to adjust. "It's only ever been you, only you." I whisper in her ear before I pull out and push in with more force.

Once her sweet heat adjusts to my cock, I pick up my pace. Her legs lock around my waist as she meets every thunderous thrust. My world spins, flying out of control. I'm falling into a blissful ecstasy that has my balls drawn up so tight, they've crawled into my abdomen.

"Fucking hell," I hiss out.

"Oh God," Paige moans out. "I'm...I'm coming!" she screams.

Paige's orgasm detonates mine. Her name rips out of my throat as white lighting blinds me and I'm rocked by aftershocks from the earth-shattering orgasm that tore through me.

We both pant for a few minutes and I do my best not to collapse onto her. I hold myself up on my elbows until I roll over to lay on my back beside her.

"Shit," Paige breathes out. Her round breasts move up and down as her chest heaves. "That was... better than my first time."

Her confession stings a little. I was her first.

"Better than your first, huh?" I play it off, smiling over at her.

"Oh shit," she jumps off the bed. "Pace was cooking dinner. And all my clothes are in the garage. What if she comes here to check on me?"

She moves to a dresser, grabs a pair of thin lace panties and glides them up her long, toned legs. My dick bobs against my stomach because—fuck me, her tits are perfect. She's bent over now, with those full, round, delectable breasts bouncing as she's getting dressed. I want to have her again and again.

"One more round." I reach down to cup my balls and hook my thumb around the root of my dick.

"As good as your dick is, I really need to go."

I blow air out, closing my eyes in defeat as I throw my head back against the bed. The scents of lavender, vanilla, and sex invade my sinuses. Opening my eyes, I find Paige standing over me and smiling, and it's like a ray sunshine—she blinds me with her beauty.

"What if I wrap my lips around the base of your big fat dick later? Would that give me a hall pass?" she teases.

I grin. "Not only would you get a hall pass, I'll put you on the dean's list. Depending on how good you can suck this big fat cock."

"Oh, I know I'll do a good job."

I raise an eyebrow. "I'll be the judge."

CHAPTER THIRTY-TWO

Paige

New beginnings was the topic of last night's grief support meeting. That's precisely what I'm dreaming of. A new beginning with Cade. It's been a week of stealing kisses, sneaking touches under a blanket, under the table. Then there's the heated, closed-door "meetings" we've been having. His body pressed into mine from behind. His cock driving into me so fast and hard, I see stars. I clench my thighs at the thought of his wickedness.

Knock, knock.

Someone is tapping on my bedroom door.

"Come in."

Cade saunters in, looking delicious in a blue dress shirt that strains to cover the span of his shoulders, and darker blue slacks that fit him in all the right places. I bite my bottom lip trying to contain the urge to bite him.

"Fuck, you look good." His deep voice vibrates through the air.

"I was thinking the same thing."

"What, that you look good?" He raises an eyebrow, teasing.

"Exactly," I tease back.

Moving behind me, he brushes my hair to one side and places small butterfly kisses along my neck.

"Cade," I try to shake him off.

"Hmm."

"I don't want my makeup or hair messed up." We're meeting Callie and Jack for dinner at The Bar and Grill. It's a new spot that opened two weeks ago. I've heard all the women at school talk about it and I've been looking forward to having an adult night. "Plus, we can't be late. I still need to run the kids to your parents' house."

Disappointment covers his face. He drops his lips, placing his forehead on my shoulder. Blowing out a breath he raises his face up.

"I'll run them over while you finish getting dressed."

I turn, placing my arms up on his shoulders while running the tips of my fingers along his neck.

"Thank you." I place a small kiss on his already pink lips.

"Just remember you owe me a blow job," he says as he backs up to leave. Holding up two fingers he says, "Two blow jobs."

I fake a gasp.

It's been an hour since Cade left for his parents' house. We were meeting Callie at seven. I glance at my watch. Seven. *Shit.*

The wood planks under my feet are worn from the pacing I've done in the living room. My gut twists with concern. I wring my fingers and continue pacing back again over the floor.

"Where are you Cade?"

He would call if something came up, wouldn't he? We've crossed a new line, one that wrapped our spirits, bound our souls into one.

My heart races at the sound of my phone ringing from my clutch. Running to it, my heels thunder in my ears.

Callie's soft voice asks, "Paige, where are you? Did you two get… side tracked?" Her approval sings in her tone.

"No, Cade dropped the kids off with your parents an hour ago but he's not back yet to pick me up. I called his cell but he's not answering. I'm getting worried."

"I'll have Jack… hold on, Mother's calling." I hear her click over.

It's as if ants are crawling along my skin. I can't stop my panicky breathing as anxiety tears at me.

"Oh god Paige, Cade's been in a wreck." Her voice trembles with fear of losing him—her last brother.

"Where?" I'm already in the garage. "Fuck," I yell. Cade took my car, leaving his Porsche at my house. I run back to the kitchen, snatch his keys off the bar where he usually leaves them, and race to his car parked in the driveway.

"On highway nine. We're headed there now."

"Meet you there." I jump into the driver's seat, press the starter and pray to God above I can remember how to drive a stick. I haven't driven one since high school.

The little black car spits and stutters while I do my best to work the gas and clutch, and reverse out of the driveway. When it comes to a roll, I push it up into first, and the gears grind and shudder underneath the car. I wince at the sound. The car finally comes to life and I head to highway nine.

A traffic jam appears as I round a sharp turn on the highway and I slow the car, pulling it onto the shoulder behind the last car in line. Parking it, I get out and break into a full run. I have to get to him. An urgency inside of me calls out, reminding me of what it is like to lose someone.

I can't lose him, not when I just found him again.

"Ma'am you can't be here," a young officer says as I step onto the glass-covered pavement. "Ma'am!" he repeats.

I ignore him because right now all that matters is that I see Cade. Touch him. Feel his warm skin against mine.

I finally reach him. "Cade." It comes out as a whisper so quiet only he could hear. One soul in need of the other soul that fulfills it.

Cade is sitting on the pavement, broken glass sprinkled around him. His head slowly turns, and he looks at me with stormy, haunted eyes. Blood coats his face, no doubt caused by cuts from the glass. My heart sinks at the sight, but I am heartened somewhat by the half-smile that forms on his still beautiful, strong face.

Dropping to my knees, I reach out to cup his face. "I was so worried." His smile is faint.

He places his hands on top of mine. "I need to tell you something. I've been fighting with myself to say it. Your first time..." He stalls.

I want to release him from his worry, tell him the secret I've been holding. The secret of the past that I've kept from everyone.

"You don't have to say anything. I know. I know it was you and not Cain. I knew it was you when I told you I wanted you to be my first." He's quiet. His lips are parted like he wants to ask me how I knew it.

"Why didn't you say anything?" he asks.

"I did... I went to Cain after a while and tried to tell him, but he stopped me from speaking. He told me that you had run off because you had gotten some girl pregnant. I was so embarrassed. Then like an idiot I let him spill lies to me. The first one was when he pretended it was him that had crawled into my room." Cade's body stiffens.

"That fucker." He says it so low it sounds dangerous.

If Cain was here, I have no doubt that Cade would kill him.

"It doesn't matter anymore. I love you, Cade."

Because of my embarrassment, I fell into the arms of the wrong boy—but that doesn't mean that I didn't grow to love him. My love for Cain did bloom, and I'm sure he loved me in his own messed up way, and we made two little souls who are my everything. Just like the man in front of me is becoming.

An officer comes over to Cade. "We'll need you to give a statement." After handing a card over to Cade, the officer walks off.

"Statement? What happened?" For the first time, I take in the accident scene. There's no car—mine or anyone else's. Just an assortment of car parts and glass covering the pavement.

"The car hit the rock hill and went down the ravine."

Standing up, I start to walk toward the edge when Cade grabs my wrist. "Don't, Paige. You don't need to see it."

"It's just a car. I'm not going to cry over it." I give a small laugh.

Pulling my hand out of his hold, I stand on the edge and peer down at the crumpled metal. I gasp at the sight of Dillion's body pinned under it, looking up at me. I stumble back.

"I was trying to spare you." Cade's breath fans across my ear as his hands turn me and I crash into his chest. His large arms wrap around me like a security blanket.

CHAPTER THIRTY-THREE

Cade

A stabbing pain shoots though my body when I try to roll over onto my left side. The emergency room nurse told me that my left shoulder and neck are completely covered with bruises, and cuts run along my face and body like skid marks. Luckily for me, they are only superficial. But they still hurt like hell. I roll back onto my back just in time to see an angel open the bedroom door and smile down at me.

After leaving the emergency room, Paige told me she wasn't going to let me out of her sight that I needed to come back to her house. I insisted that I was fine but like the wonderfully stubborn woman she is, she wouldn't take any excuses. So... I did what I was told and stayed here last night.

Her mouth pulls back like she's the one in pain.

"What is it?" I ask, even though I know it's the sight of my face and bruises that has her drawing back like someone punched her in the stomach.

I haven't seen my face, but I can feel the scrapes along my forehead and cheeks. The bruises must be deep, given the sharp pain that travels straight to the bone when I move or touch them. I avoided any mirrors last night, so I haven't assessed the damage. "Is it really that bad?" Even speaking stings.

"Your face looks like someone took pleasure in beating the crap out of you."

"They did. Damn airbags," I wince. Pain. Damn.

"Can you sit up?"

Doing my best to push though the soreness, I wiggle around until I've propped myself against the headboard of the bed.

"Here," Paige sets a tray down with a plate of breakfast fare—omelet, toast, and bacon. My last meal was yesterday, so I'm hungry, and my mouth waters.

After she sets the tray down, she gathers the pillows on the bed. "Lean forward," she commands. I gingerly do as I'm told, and she places the pillows behind my back. My heart grows larger for this woman who's looking after me, going over and beyond what is necessary.

Once she finishes making sure I'm comfortable, she picks up my fork, scooping up a bite of the omelet.

"Paige, I can feed myself," I tell her as I place my hand over hers that's holding the fork. "I've got this." She scolds at me but lets go of the fork.

She gives a deep sigh then looks around the room. I can see she has something on her mind but she's afraid to tell me what it is.

"Sit down and talk to me about what's on that pretty mind of yours." I stab my omelet, gathering more than a forkful and stuffing it into my mouth. I moan at the deliciousness.

Fuck. So good!

The omelet is filled with peppers, onions, and some kind of seasoning that has garlic in it. So damn good.

Paige lets out a cute laugh before her face turns serious

again, like she forgot for a moment that she was about to get down to business. Only this time, when her face turns serious, my senses go on alert. The soft easiness that filled the air a second ago is gone and it's replaced by a stiffness that could suffocate me.

She clears her throat. "I need to talk to you about last night." Her eyes bore into me, searching for answers. "You said before that you were into some... shady stuff but you didn't go into detail." She pauses for a beat. "I care about you, Cade, and I don't want to have to look over my shoulder, not for me, not for my kids, and I don't want to have to wonder if you're going to make it home."

My eyes turn down to my plate, bile rising up from the pit of my stomach. I hate that there's even a fraction of her that feels the need to have this talk. That she saw Dillion laying lifeless, his eyes staring up, laughter in them as if he was still trying to destroy what progress I have made in a relationship with Paige.

"I know," my voice is small as the hope of an *us* fades out of my reach.

She places her small, delicate hand on my knee. A simple touch that sends a fire though my veins. I raise my head, locking eyes with her. How she fights the suffocating air to speak shows how strong she truly is.

"Doesn't mean I don't want you or want to be with you. I... just need to know whatever it was you were involved in won't have consequences. The part you took. I didn't ask questions last night because I knew it was all too much to take in. Especially after seeing Dillion looking up at me." An emotion of dread flashes in her eyes like she hates that she looked over the edge last night and saw Dillion, like she should have listened and took heed of my warning to spare her the memory of looking death in the face. "I want complete honesty if there is going to be an us," she flicks her finger between us. "There was no honesty with Cain and I *won't* repeat that pattern. You need to be honest with me about everything."

I inhale. Taking a deep breath, I prepare myself for her to think the worst of me when I tell her my darkest secrets.

I'm not sure if the tightness in my lungs is from the general stiffness of my body or if it's from fear, but my chest loosens up just enough so that I can speak. I begin to tell her everything. How killing or punishing those who abuse children or their spouses became normal. How it felt good to take someone's life. How it gave me the release I needed.

I told her how it all started when my friend took his own life because his father was abusing him. Then I spoke of saving Dillion in the alley when he was getting the crap beaten out of him by a drug dealer. How, years later, when the drug dealer and I crossed paths again, and he knew I was going to kill him, he told me of Dillion's betrayal. That Dillion had been sleeping with his wife, Honey, and stealing from his stash of dope. That the only reason I believed him was because I remembered a woman named Honey coming around to suck Dillion off. That for months afterward I laid awake at night wishing I hadn't saved that fucker Dillion's life. How I should have let him meet his demise. If there is one thing I hate more than anything it's a cheater—just like Cain.

Then I finally told her about my own drug use. How I was at my lowest point because of Cain and how nothing mattered. Nothing but wanting to numb the pain I felt from losing everything I had known.

"Cade, I'm so sorry."

"You didn't know."

I set the tray aside and pull her to me. "I'm here now and everything is in the past where it belongs. I don't want my past to own me anymore. I want to focus on what's going to be, starting now." I wrap myself around her as best I can, managing to move my sore shoulders enough to enclose her completely in my embrace. We fit perfectly together. With her in my arms, I feel as if I've found the missing puzzle piece of my soul, of my life,

I feel unbroken.

She pulls her head back to look up at me. I still can see some hesitation in her eyes.

"Do you think there are going to be more problems in the future? Do you think anyone will be coming after you or seeking revenge?"

Staring in her eyes I want to tell her *no*, but the truth is, I can't guarantee what the future holds. So I give her the truth.

"Dillion is the only one that knew my identity. We were close at one time—like brothers. He's the only one I trusted enough to tell everything to." *Although trusting him was a mistake.* "I can't guarantee that someone in the future won't find out about my past, but I can promise you that I'll defend you with my life. If anyone tries to hurt you or the children, I won't hesitate a second to kill them. You already have my heart and I'll love you till my dying day."

She sighs in contentment against my chest, and it vibrates all the way to my dick. I roll us down onto the bed, almost knocking over the tray of food. She laughs and right at that moment the door bursts open and three little rug rats come rushing in to jump into bed with us.

CHAPTER THIRTY-FOUR

Paige

Cade and I have been inseparable, and the kids enjoy having him around—especially now that he's completely healed and gets on the floor to play with them.

The doorbell rings.

"I'll get it," I yell out as I wipe my hands on a kitchen towel.

When I open the door, I see a man in a brown uniform standing on my porch.

"Paige Staton?"

I nod. "The one and only," I joke with a smile.

His face is devoid of any expression. My teasing him hasn't made a dent in his seriousness.

All business like, he hands over a tablet and says, "Need your signature."

My eyebrows draw up. "What am I signing for?" I'm confused because there's not a package in his hands or on the porch.

"I have an envelope." He reaches behind his back and passes me a folded up white envelope that he must have had shoved in his back pocket. *How unprofessional.*

In the upper left corner of the envelope is written *Cain Staton*. The stranger walks off and I don't waste any time before tearing open the envelope and pulling out a single sheet of paper.

It's a fucking letter from Cain with a picture attached of a much younger and skinnier Cade. He's laying on a mattress looking peacefully asleep—except I suspect that he's not asleep. He has a needle in his arm and there's no explanation possible other than he was injecting poison into his body. I would be in shock if Cade hadn't already been honest with me about his previous drug use.

I storm inside, grabbing my keys off the hook where they hang by the garage door.

"I need to run an errand," I yell out to Cade. He's seated at the table painting with the kids.

He jerks his head up and his face is outlined with concern.

"Don't. Don't say anything. I need to have closure on something. I'll be right back."

Jumping into my new van, I start the car and race down the highway. I need to tell him exactly how I feel.

When I pull up at the cemetery, I throw the van into park and stomp to the single tombstone. My pulse is racing as I move closer to my destination. To the man that I refuse to let manipulate me from the grave any longer.

When I finally stand in front of the marble stone I scoff at the words, *Loving husband.*

What a fool I was. Just another pawn in his game of having his way. Always wanting to feel superior to others.

"You thought this letter," I shake the paper at the tombstone, "would make me turn away from Cade."

The words on the plain sheet of paper are in Cain's own handwriting. *He's not the person he says he is.*

"No more. You don't get to control me from your grave. You don't get to direct my life." My voice is shaky as I address the cold stone standing in front of me. "If it wasn't for your children, I would *never* speak your name." I'm sure I sound and look like a mad woman. My arms swing around as my voice becomes stone cold. So frigid that I start to feel the frostbite at the tip of my tongue for a second before it's warmed by the hot boiling blood pumping from my heart. Aggression seeps out of my pores as I raise my foot and kick his tombstone, almost sending it tumbling backwards.

I take the note and the picture and tear them into tiny pieces, letting them drop to the ground. They scatter across Cain's grave, some of the pieces dance away as if they, too, want to be as far away from his grave as possible. Hope fills me that they will decompose into nothingness along with memories of Cain's betrayal and controlling ways.

Feeling the sourness start to ease from my heart, I say my final goodbyes to Cain.

"I won't be back. Not till this bitterness leaves me. Your children will only be sheltered from your deceitful ways till they get older. I refuse to make you out to be greater than you were. And I will do everything in my power to have them grow up to be like Cade." Turning and walking back to my car, I hurry to make it home.

As I enter the house, I find Cade, Ivory, Jameson, and Kip all working at the kitchen table just like I left them. I walk up behind Cade and wrap my arms around him.

"You made it back," he says in that rough voice of his.

"Yes," I whisper. "I'm right where I belong."

Epilogue

Cade

The sunlight breaks in the room, shining on the hair of two little runts in their cribs. Blond hair, the color of gold, sparkling in the sunlight.

"Dada," they both call out when they spot me.

"I'm here." My voice is gritty from the lack of sleep.

Having fifteen-month-old twins is a damn cluster fuck. Staggering over, I lift Sadie out first then walk over to the next crib and toss Seven under my arm. "Oh my goodness, you both are getting so big. But why can't you sleep longer? Mommy and Daddy need their rest," I say as I walk us into the master bedroom where Paige is still sleeping. I get back into the bed and let the little monsters loose to climb around. Paige rolls over with sleep still in her eyes. Her full tits almost spill out of her small tank. Seven slaps his little palm against one of them.

"Hey now. That's mine." He looks at me, smiling and bouncing on his behind.

Little hellion.

Paige chuckles at me staking my ownership.

Life is good these days. The brightness that I feel from the ray of sunshine laying beside me warms my heart. Paige is everything—the beat to my heart, the breath in my lungs. Her very being brings salvation to my soul.

"The others will be up soon," Paige says, running her hand though Sadie's little blonde curls. Sadie pushes her brother out of the way to be closer to her mommy.

Sadie's caramel eyes watch her mother adoringly while Seven climbs over me. His boney knees stab me in my side.

"I might as well get up because these two, especially this little monster—" I toss Seven down on the bed, pretending to body slam him. He breaks out in a full giggle. "Will not go back to sleep."

"Hmm," Paige's eyes close as a soft snore slips out.

Fuck me, she's beautiful.

Pushing off the bed, I toss Seven over my shoulder and we head to the kitchen. His giggles send my heart soaring over the edge of a cliff… every time.

"Hey, Cade," Kip says from the couch.

"Hey, are you the only one up?"

"Yep," he replies. "Are you making breakfast before my game?"

"Heck, yeah." I pump a fist in the air. "We've got to keep up that strength so you can kick some butt."

His grin is infectious.

Dropping Seven down beside Kip, I stroll to the kitchen to make everyone a hearty breakfast.

"Come on. My grandmother can coach better than that," I yell. "Coach Smith sucks." Paige tugs at my arm.

"Sit down, Cade. You're embarrassing Kip." Her voice is quiet, her eyes avoiding contact with the other parents sitting around us.

"I can't help it if his coach SUCKS BUTT!" I yell the last part.

"Stop it," Paige hisses.

"Sucks butt." Seven repeats what I said, making Ivory and Jameson laugh while Paige sends me a scowl.

I point my finger at Seven. "Don't repeat what I say." I tell him that, even knowing that it won't do much good.

The game ends, ending the biggest losing streak in Haydenville.

"Our coach sucks," Kip says in disappointment.

"I know, buddy." I throw my hand on his shoulder.

"Sucks butt," Seven chirps again.

"Ugh, impossible," Paige mutters.

I'm sure she's talking about Seven's comment, but my mind goes in a different direction. This life, what I have now with Paige, seemed an impossible dream. Always out of reach for me until… fate took charge.

I'd just dropped off all three kids at my parents' house and I'm walking back to the car. Excitement is pumping through my veins, and I want to skip like a child. I plan to be alone with Paige all night tonight, with a good portion of that time spent with my cock buried in her.

When I get back to Paige's SUV, I buckle myself in and start the car.

The car revs louder when my eagerness to dip my dick into Paige has me stepping on the gas a little too hard. I ease up a bit to be sure I get back to her in one piece.

A sharp edge presses into my neck.

"Tsk tsk, you didn't do your job." Dillion's raspy voice scratches my eardrum.

I grit my teeth. Mother fucker.

"Should've done the job, Loverboy. Did you think you could just walk away to your happily ever after?"

"He's your fucking half-brother. Not our normal victim." I grip the steering wheel so hard my knuckles are white.

"He's an ass. Beating his wife every spare moment."

I was there—I know he's lying. If anything, the wife was the one that needed to be taken out. I keep my mouth shut as I accelerate around the curves in the road.

"Slow down," Dillion demands, pressing the knife a little harder into my neck.

The sharp edge slices into the delicate flesh and I feel blood trickling down my neck.

I press harder on the gas, driving even faster. A yellow sign flashes a warning about the sharp curve ahead.

The only way out is to take him out. I keep accelerating, increasing my chances of ending this madness. I turn the wheel as Dillion spits profanity at me. My Porsche would handle this curve just fine, but I'm counting on Paige's SUV not being nearly so nimble.

I'm right—the car isn't able to make it. The wheels scar up the pavement as I lose control. The vehicle shrieks and Dillion screams as the car flips over and over on the pavement and then the shoulder, before it plunges into a ravine.

My body is suspended in the air, held upside down by my seat belt, my protector. Blood coats my face making everything I see hazy. Reaching down, I manage to unbuckle myself, falling with a thump. Fuck, that hurt. Broken glass surrounds me and cuts into my hands as I crawl my way out and away.

I haven't gone but a few feet when my eyes widen in disbelief. Dillion. He must have been thrown from the car. He's lying here, his limbs at odd angles and his eyes staring up at me.

"Help me." His voice is a whisper in the darkness.

I grin knowing he's completely… fucked.

"May you rest in hell, fucker," I pray over him as I snap his neck.

"Cade," Kip says, pulling me back to the present.

"Yeah, buddy."

"When we get home. Will you play Motorfest with me?"

I clap him on the shoulder. "I have to warn you. I'm really good at racing."

When we get to Paige's van, we load up all the kids. Climbing behind the wheel, I adjust the mirror to see all the small faces behind me—the children that tie us together. Cain, Kellie, me, and Paige. We're all bound together because the love we have for these children surpasses any wrong we've done. They don't deserve to be punished for our shortcomings. They deserve all the love we have to offer them.

My beautiful wife touches my arm, "You ready?"

Giving her a smirk, I let her know, "I'm always ready." I wiggle my eyebrows.

About

International Best Selling Author

Aurelia writes contemporary and dark romance. She enjoys reading it just as much! She lives in Alabama with her husband, daughter and fur babies. She spends most of her time taking care of her loved ones and plotting stories. Aurelia is excited to share her stories with you!

Find out more-Follow Aurelia on

Www.Aureliayatesauthor.com

Instagram

(20) Facebook

Amazon.com: Aurelia Yates: books, biography, latest update